DAKOTA HEAT, VOLUME 1

Her Dakota Men
Dakota Ranch Crude

Leah Brooke

MENAGE AMOUR

Siren Publishing, Inc.
www.SirenPublishing.com

A SIREN PUBLISHING BOOK
IMPRINT: Ménage Amour

DAKOTA HEAT, VOLUME 1
Her Dakota Men
Dakota Ranch Crude
Copyright © 2009 by Leah Brooke

ISBN-10: 1-60601-525-7
ISBN-13: 978-1-60601-525-4

First Printing: November 2009

Cover design by Jinger Heaston
All cover art and logo copyright © 2009 by Siren Publishing, Inc.

Printed in the U.S.A.

PUBLISHER
Siren Publishing, Inc.
www.SirenPublishing.com

DEDICATIONS

Her Dakota Men
Thanks to my family for their encouragement and to Diana for her
continuous support.

Dakota Ranch Crude
To Frank and Angelo. Thanks for the love and support.

Leah Brooke

Siren Publishing

Ménage Amour

Her Dakota Men

Leah Brooke

HER DAKOTA MEN

Dakota Heat Anthology 1

LEAH BROOKE
Copyright © 2009

Chapter One

Stacy Daniels listened to the minister as she looked down at the coffin. Whether Benton Daniels, her father, had gone to heaven or hell she had no idea. She could hardly believe that a man like him would die of anything as small as a clogged artery.

No, men like Benton Daniels died in stampedes, tornados, or breaking wild horses. Men like Benton Daniels loomed larger than life and dominated their surroundings.

Her father had been a bear of a man. Standing head and shoulders above most men, he'd always been strong as an ox and twice as mean. His deep booming voice carried and could be heard far away, so he didn't have to raise it. But he did.

She looked now across to her father's friends and neighbors. She saw pity in their eyes when they looked at her and she knew stories of her father's mistreatment had reached them. It didn't surprise her. Word got around fast in ranch circles, and her father certainly hadn't tried to be discreet. No one cried, not even her. Her father had been dead to her for a long time. Nevertheless, it had been a shock as she'd realized how much his death would change her life. She had moments when she thought she would crumble at any moment.

She drew her strength from the men standing behind her. Ever since she'd come home, at least one of them had always been in earshot in case she needed anything. They made the ranch a safe haven for her, because she knew they would always be there if she needed them.

The minister concluded the service, and she moved forward to place the single rose on her father's coffin. She wanted to fling it, but didn't. She mourned the way her life would change more than she mourned her father. She turned away from the coffin and started back toward the road. Before she could take a second step, a hand gripped her elbow to steady her. Cash. How she knew who it was without looking, she had no idea, but she did.

Others followed suit and before she knew it they'd gotten into Wolfe's truck and headed back to the ranch. She smiled when she saw Rosa getting into Rex's truck for the ride back. Leaning her head back against the seat, she sighed. She dreaded the next few hours. Everyone would be coming to the house to pay their condolences. She didn't want to see the pity on their faces or answer a lot of questions about what she would do now. She just didn't want to face it.

Strangely, she'd never thought about what would happen when Benton Daniels died. It just never seemed like a possibility for her. Her father seemed like the type that would be around forever.

She would have to stay a few days to do any necessary paperwork before getting back to her receptionist job in Great Falls. The dental office she worked in hadn't been her first choice but she'd needed to pay the rent.

"Are you okay, baby?"

Stacy looked up and met Wolfe's eyes in the rearview mirror. He had a predator's eyes, deep gray and slightly hooded, always watchful. She'd seen ice form in those eyes more than once and knew it could chill to the bone, but never when he'd looked at her.

"I'm fine, thanks. It was a nice turnout, wasn't it? Dad would have liked it."

Travis sat with her in the back seat and reached for her hand. "Yeah, Ben would have loved having a crowd."

Stacy turned at his sarcasm, trying to ignore the effect his touch had on her. "That's true."

Travis opened his mouth to say something but after glancing at Wolfe, closed it again. His silver eyes held hers for several moments before he spoke. "How does it feel to be back?"

She shrugged. "Strange. I wish I could attribute the pitying looks I get to dad's death but they're the same every time I come back." She pulled her hand from his as unobtrusively as possible. It had become hard to sit here and talk to them when just the touch of any one of them could make her forget what she'd been saying. "Thankfully, a few more hours of it and I'll be done. When I meet with dad's attorney tomorrow, I'll sign whatever's necessary and head for home."

"This is your home," Wolfe growled as the others frowned at her.

"This hasn't been my home for a long time."

"That's because your father was here. He's gone now. What about the ranch?"

"What about it?"

Travis shot a glance at his brother then looked back at her. "Honey, you can't just walk away from the ranch. You love the ranch."

Stacy smiled sadly. "I can't stay. It's not my home anymore."

Wolfe pulled onto the road leading to the ranch and met her eyes in the mirror again. "What are you talking about, sweetheart? Of course the ranch is your home."

Stacy shrugged and looked out the window. "I really don't feel like talking about it right now."

Thankfully they dropped the subject and made the rest of the drive in silence.

* * * *

Stacy waved the last of the mourners off, leaning back wearily against Wolfe. Realizing what she'd done, she straightened and stepped away, only to be pulled back against him again.

"Lean on me, sweetheart. We're all here for you."

All three of them had hovered over her all afternoon, and she'd been grateful for their presence. It had been an exhausting day but now she just wanted some time alone.

After what she'd told them in the truck, they'd kept eyeing each other, and then her but she didn't know what they'd been looking for. Silent messages passed between them but she had no clue what they'd meant and didn't want to ask. They hadn't again mentioned the ranch to her.

"Would you like to go for a ride?" Wolfe asked against her hair.

Stacy turned and smiled faintly. "That would be great. Let me go get changed." Her breath caught as he leaned down to kiss her forehead.

 He straightened and lifted her chin with his finger. "The ride will do you good. Everything will be fine now, sweetheart. Benton can't hurt you anymore." He smiled tenderly and her heart did a flip. "I'll get the horses saddled. Come out when you're ready."

Standing in front of her mirror a few minutes later, Stacy regarded her reflection with amusement. She certainly didn't look like she normally did. Her blonde hair wasn't pulled tight into its usual twist. Instead it hung loose around her shoulders. Well-worn jeans replaced the office clothing she normally wore. Her blue eyes sparkled with excitement. She felt a twinge of guilt to be happy about something on the day she buried her father.

She realized how her father's very existence had been like a dark cloud hanging over her. But she loved the ranch, and a chance to ride it again made her happy. It also made her happy to be around the Dakota men again. She hadn't wanted to admit that even to herself but that didn't make it any less true. She sank down onto the bed.

She'd spent the last three days thinking about what she should do. She'd thought of little else since Wolfe had come to inform her of her father's death and bring her back to the ranch.

Wanting to remain here more than anything, she knew she couldn't.

How could she when she loved three men who lived here? She'd never be able to stay without hurting all of them. Wolfe, Travis and Cash didn't deserve to be hurt that way.

So, she had to leave.

She couldn't leave and expect them and their father Rex, the ranch foreman, to run the ranch indefinitely. That left only one option.

She had to make arrangements to sell the ranch, the only place she'd ever found happiness. Then she could leave.

It saddened her to think that she'd never see the ranch again. Wolfe, Travis and Cash, along with Rex and Rosa, would have to find work elsewhere, and she'd probably never see any of them ever again. Her father would probably laugh in his grave to see her so miserable. Moving to her window, she looked down to see that Wolfe waited outside and had already saddled a horse for her.

Her eyes caressed him. He'd changed into his jeans and work shirt. He and his brothers sure did know how to fill out some work clothes. Years of working the ranch had toned their bodies into works of art. They all had brown, sun-streaked hair, and of course, Cash had let his grow too long again. They had varying shades of gray eyes, which today had seemed to settle on her more often than usual.

She turned from the window. Right now they liked and respected her. She had to leave before she lost even that. If she stayed, she would end up killing their feelings for her and would more than likely cause a rift between the brothers, not to mention how disappointed Rex and Rosa would be with her. She had to leave and never come back. That was the only way.

Going down to the kitchen, she paused at the stove, leaning over Rosa's shoulder. "Why are you cooking? The neighbors brought all kinds of food."

Rosa automatically raised the spoon she'd been using to stir the contents of the big pot to give Stacy a taste. "Now that your daddy's gone, Rex and the boys eat at the house. Those boys like my cooking. When they get done working, they're going to want something that fills them up. Lenore brought that stupid casserole of hers. My boys don't want her casserole. They like my beef stew and biscuits. So do you."

Rosa turned and Stacy was surprised by the sheen of tears in her eyes before the older woman embraced her. "Your father never let you ride, did he, honey? Every time he caught you, he'd make you come inside and help me with dinner."

Stacy's vision blurred as she hugged Rosa back. "Wolfe, Travis and Cash used to sneak me out or I never would have been able to ride. You always covered for me."

Rosa straightened and wiped her eyes with her apron. "Well, we don't have to sneak around anymore. Now get on out of here before Wolfe comes looking for you and takes up all the room in my kitchen."

"Yes, ma'am." Stacy gave Rosa a peck on the cheek and headed outside. Rosa had been a mother to her since she was born and being away from her had been difficult. Knowing that after the ranch sold she'd probably never see her again made her eyes well up again. She found her hat in its usual place on the rack and headed outside. No matter how long she'd been gone, Rosa never moved her things.

Wolfe smiled as soon as he saw her. "I was beginning to think that I would have to come and get you."

"I stopped in the kitchen. Rosa is busy cooking." Before she could get her foot in the stirrup, Wolfe lifted her onto the saddle. His hands lingered on her thighs before he handed her the reins. She trembled at his touch. Her nipples beaded almost immediately. She shifted the reins, hoping he didn't notice her reaction.

He mounted his own horse. "Why is she cooking? There's enough food in the refrigerator to feed an army."

"Yes, but it's not her cooking. Her boys don't want any of Lenore's stupid casserole," she mimicked.

He smiled as expected. Neither of them spoke for a while as they rode, enjoying the scenery. She missed this place so much. The fences had been kept in good shape and everything looked well cared for. It should sell fast. They rode in silence, usually side by side, but there had been a few places that they'd had to ride single file.

She appreciated the silence as she knew he did. Like his father, he didn't feel the need to talk constantly or loudly. He probably knew she'd needed a little peace after the day they'd all had. She appreciated his consideration. Her dad's friends and neighbors had made more than one comment about her moving back to the ranch, and she'd muttered something non committal and changed the subject. She could just imagine the looks on the other ranchers' faces if she told them she couldn't stay because she had fallen in love with three men. She could just imagine the looks on Wolfe, Travis and Cash's faces.

"Do you remember Baby?"

Stacy's lips twitched when she remembered the time Wolfe had carried in a newborn calf, half frozen. Its mother had died in the snowstorm, and luckily they'd found the calf lying next to its mother before it met the same fate.

Wolfe had carried it into the lodge where hot food and coffee had been set up. The ranch hands had been in and out all day, warming up with a hot meal and coffee before heading back out into the cold again. Stacy had only been sixteen then and had been helping Rosa and Will, the ranch cook, to keep up with the staggering amount of food and coffee needed.

When Wolfe walked in, carrying the calf, she'd run over to him. "Is he still alive?"

Wolfe, in his sheerling jacket had looked larger than life carrying the calf, both of them covered with ice and snow. "He won't be for long if we don't get him warmed up."

He'd carried the poor calf close to the huge fireplace, and Stacy had grabbed a towel and followed. Kneeling next to the calf, she began to briskly rub him down, trying to dry him off and get him warm.

Cash had come in soon after with a bottle of warm milk. Stacy fed the calf while the men took over rubbing him dry.

Travis had walked in, his face grim. "We lost the other one on the way in."

Kneeling in front of the fire, bottle feeding a half frozen calf, Stacy had looked up. The fire had back-dropped the men. The sight of the three of them standing in front of it had taken her breath away. Dizzy with unfamiliar emotions racing through her, she realized she had fallen in love.

All three had stared at her in a way that made her heart flutter. An unexpected and unfamiliar feeling of hunger had built inside her that had nothing to do with food. Her heart raced and she became light headed and tingly.

Her father had walked in just then, loud and irate as usual. She'd looked away but not before seeing the way they glared at him. Rage had shone in their eyes before being quickly extinguished.

The spell had been broken but from that day on, she recognized the futility of loving the three men that had become such a big part of her life.

She smiled at Wolfe. "I remember Baby."

Wolfe grinned. "He used to follow you around like a puppy. He ran over anybody standing in his way when he saw you."

"He liked me."

"You used to pet him and talk to him all the time."

Stacy nodded and looked over at him. "I remember how you, your brothers and Rex used to keep him in the closest pasture. You watched out for him because you knew I would be heartbroken if anything happened to him."

"We didn't do a very good job of it, did we?"

Stacy shrugged. "It wasn't your fault. I should have known that if my father knew I got attached to anything, he would get rid of it."

Wolfe's face tightened. "Yeah, but to sell Baby off that way and rush to tell you that he'd be slaughtered for veal was just plain mean. You cried for days."

Wolfe Travis and Cash had all tried to comfort her but she'd already begun to shy away from them. She no longer trusted her feeling for them and was afraid that if her father knew they were important to her, he would get rid of them just as easily as he'd gotten rid of Baby.

"That's when I really began to hate my father. I knew then that I'd leave right after I graduated from high school."

They rode in silence for several more minutes.

"Rosa really misses you."

"I really miss her, too."

"We all really miss you."

She looked over at him to find him watching her intently. Her eyes slid to where his hands gripped the reins and couldn't help but imagine them on her body. His jean-clad thighs looked thick with muscle as he rode, and she couldn't help but wonder what it would feel like to have those thighs spreading hers to move between them. Years of ranch work had made his arms into ropes of muscle. She'd seen him and his brothers use that muscle to train horses, had seen them lift sacks of feed and could only imagine how it would feel to have arms such as those around her.

She'd met several men in Great Falls, had even dated a few but none of them could hold a candle to these three. Every time one of them would try to touch her, she had seen the Dakota men's' faces and had been unable to give them what they wanted. She'd never felt even an inkling of desire for another man. She'd probably spend her life alone now and that depressed her even more. She wanted them.

"Stacy?"

Damn. He'd caught her staring. She lifted her gaze to his eyes. "Sorry, my mind wandered. What did you say?"

He smiled at her as though he knew what she'd been thinking. Her face burned. "I said that we all miss you."

"I miss all of you, too." Surprised when her eyes welled again, she looked straight ahead. The scenery blurred as her eyes filled with tears.

He moved close and touched her arm. "Stacy, honey, what's wrong?"

Her eyes involuntarily slid to his, and she heard him curse. Pulling on his reins, he grabbed hers out of her hands. He pulled her from her saddle to his lap smoothly, and she wondered absently what kind of strength it would take to do that.

Once the tears started they would no longer be held back, and she began to cry in earnest. Wolfe's arms went around her as he pulled her tightly against his chest. It felt so good to be held this way, as if nothing in the world could hurt her. Surrounded by heat and strength, she came undone.

She held on tightly, her tears soaking his shirt, but she couldn't stop. She'd missed them all so much. She loved them all so much. She loved her home and now she had to sell it. Her father had never wanted her, and even Rosa and Rex would be lost to her forever. The few friends she'd made in Great Falls could never take the place of all that. Why did she have to fall in love with all of them? Why did she have to be so selfish? It broke her heart that she would lose them all with her selfishness but she couldn't seem to do anything about it.

Wolfe moved but she didn't care as long as he held her. He never tried to shush her or tell her to stop crying. He simply held her and let her cry it out. His arms stayed wrapped around her, and he rocked her as he would a child. His lips touched her hair and she clutched him harder. It seemed like hours before her sobs lessened and then stopped altogether, and she leaned against him exhausted.

"Feel better, sweetheart?"

Embarrassed, she looked up and saw him leaning over her with a handkerchief. Nodding, she reached for it only to have him grasp her hand in his. Her turned it to touch his lips to her palm and lowered her hand and began wiping the tears from her face.

"I'm sorry. I don't know what got into me."

"You've had a rough day, haven't you, honey?"

Stacy looked around in surprise to see that she was settled on Wolfe's lap under a tree. The horses wandered nearby. She knew the horses wouldn't go far, and if they did, Wolfe, Travis and Cash's had been trained to come at their whistle.

When Wolfe finished mopping her face, Stacy tried to extricate herself from his embrace. He pulled her back down, and she wearily leaned against him. She would lean on him and pretend nothing was wrong, if only for a little while.

"Are you okay now?"

The heat from his big body wrapped around her from behind. She kept looking out, seeing the mountains in the distance. "I'm fine. Like you said, it's been a rough day."

"You like it here, don't you?"

Stacy nodded, keeping her eyes forward. "It's beautiful here. What's not to like?"

His hands on her waist, hot and hard, made her jittery. God, she loved having him wrapped around her this way. He bent his head, and touched his lips to her neck. "Then why don't you stay?"

Oh how she would love to be able to do that. But loving all three of them would eventually destroy it all. Stacy closed her eyes as a wave of longing washed over her. "I can't." She gasped when he started unbuttoning her shirt. She put her hands over his to stop him, but it didn't even slow him down. "What are you doing?"

"I'm going to try to change your mind."

"Oh, God. Please, you shouldn't." But even she heard the longing in her voice.

He had already unbuttoned enough of the buttons to slide his hands inside her shirt and undo the front clasp of her bra. His hands felt hot and rough against her breasts as he cupped them.

Her head fell back on his shoulder as his lips moved over her neck. Tingles of pleasure ran down her neck from where his lips touched and shot straight to her breasts. Her nipples had turned into hard little pebbles that just ached to be rubbed. Moisture flowed from her slit, and her stomach clenched as fierce need clawed at her. Her hands gripped his thick forearms.

"If that's not beautiful, I don't know what is," he murmured against her neck. "Look at how delicate your breasts look in my hands."

She looked down, and another jolt of lust shot through her. His large tanned hands looked huge on her pale breasts. As she watched, he pinched a nipple, and she gasped at the exquisite sensation.

"Stay, baby. I'll take good care of you, I promise."

She wanted to say yes more than she wanted to draw her next breath. "I can't," she whimpered. He turned her, lifting her, rubbing his lips over her breast before sucking a nipple into his mouth. Straddling his thighs, she gripped his shoulder tightly, feeling the play of muscles as he moved. With the other hand she gripped his head, holding it to her breast. She'd never been touched so intimately before, and a firestorm began to rage within her. The tug on her nipples shot between her thighs. She pulled him harder against her. His hand moved to the fastening of her jeans, and she couldn't have stopped him for anything. He lifted her, laying her across his lap and sliding her jeans down to her knees. The cool air outside did nothing to cool the heat at her slit.

He watched her face as he slid a thick finger through her folds. "You're already wet for me, aren't you, sweetheart?"

"Oh God. Yes." He touched her right where the sensations had gathered.

She cried out at the rough thickness of his finger pushing into her. The slight burning sensation made her hiss.

"You're still a virgin?"

"Yes. Oh!"

"Good girl. I've waited for years for you to come back here to stay, and I'd wondered if you let somebody take you. I've had nightmares about it, Stacy." He pressed again. "Please tell me this is mine to take."

"Yes, please. I can't stand it."

He removed his hand to pull off her boots so he could slide her jeans and panties off. He tossed them aside and sitting back against the tree with her in his lap, began to run his hands all over her. His eyes held hers as he traced his fingers lightly over her breasts. "You are the most beautiful woman in the world to me. Look at you."

She flushed under his gaze, holding on tightly to his shoulders as he caressed her.

Wolfe groaned. "I've never in my life wanted a woman as much as I want you."

She dropped her head onto his shoulder and began to unbutton his shirt, shivering under his hands.

"Are you cold, little one?" He took off his jacket and wrapped it around her back.

"No," she smiled at him shyly. "Just the opposite." She finally had enough buttons undone to push her hands inside. She loved the feel of his springy chest hair under her hands and the play of muscles beneath it.

"You're not leaving the ranch again, Stacy. I've waited forever for you to grow up. This is your home. I want you to stay."

"I don't want to talk about it now. Kiss me. Take me."

Wolfe took her mouth with his in a kiss unlike any other she'd ever had. The soft, teasing kisses she'd had from the men she'd dated were all but forgotten as Wolfe claimed her mouth with his own. Fire raced through her blood as his firm sensual lips demanded a response, his tongue taking possession of her mouth and making it his. He didn't play or tease or ask. He took, and she gave.

His hand moved back down to her folds, and she parted her legs wide to give him whatever he wanted. She knew he could satisfy this incredible need.

He rolled her clit, and her body tightened as she shook in reaction. He picked her up and deposited her on the soft grass nearby, making sure the jacket protected her from the hard ground. He lifted his mouth from hers to suck a nipple into it. "I love these little nipples."

She arched, pushing her breast harder against his mouth.

"Do you want it harder, sweetheart? I don't want to hurt you."

"Yes, I don't know, anything."

When his teeth scraped her nipple, she froze. She cried out, her voice loud in the air.

"You like that little bite of pain, don't you, sweetheart?"

"Oh! I shouldn't. Why?"

"Because you're perfect, that's why. I've always known you would be like this." He reached down to pinch her folds lightly. "If you'd given your virginity to someone else I would have beaten your ass raw."

He drew a deep breath, his wide shoulders trembling under her hands. He lowered his forehead to hers. "Oh God, honey. Thank you for saving yourself." He lifted his head and smiled at her tenderly, tracing her lips with his thumb. "Your virginity is the most precious gift I'll ever receive."

Wolfe moved over her and unfastened his jeans. "I've waited years for this, Stacy. Years."

His thick length started to press into her, and she gripped him tightly. "I want you so much. Please take me."

He surged into her in one smooth thrust, and she cried out at the brief flash of pain. His big body shook as he held himself completely still inside her, staring down at her with a look on his face she had never seen before. His face looked tight, almost tortured but his eyes had become hot and hungry, more possessive than she had ever seen them.

He started to move, watching her face the entire time. When her eyes started to flutter closed, he growled.

"No. You keep your eyes open. Look at me. You're mine, Stacy. I want all of you."

Stacy couldn't deny him anything. As he moved inside her, she found herself caught in some kind of spell. It was all so intimate, so erotic, and so raw.

His body thrust deeply inside her own, and he watched every play of emotion on her face as he took her. He nudged a place inside her that made her cry out again. The reality of finally having this man inside her made her heart soar, but the feel of him had her gasping in pleasure.

Nothing in her life had prepared her for this, and she knew she would cherish this memory forever. She trembled all over, the sensations too exquisite to bear. Her body tightened more and more and a rush of pleasure washed over her, gripping her tightly in its grasp and she could do nothing to stop it.

She clenched tightly on the thickness inside her, sending a new rush over her and she screamed at the unbelievable pleasure. Wolfe increased his pace and heard him growl deep in his throat as he held himself pushed to the hilt inside her, touching her womb. Not knowing what to do, she could only hold on and trust that he would help her as the waves of pleasure seemed never ending.

She thrilled as his big body shook from the pleasure he'd found in her body, and she wrapped her arms around him, holding him close for as long as she could.

Several minutes passed as she held him, and their trembles diminished. When he lifted his head, she touched his face lovingly. If she had to sell and leave the ranch, at least she had been able to have this with him, to give this to him.

When he cupped her face, she automatically turned her cheek into his rough hand. "You are absolutely exquisite, little one." He ran his thumb over her lips, and she licked it without thinking. "Yes, absolutely exquisite."

She shivered as the air cooled her body.

"Come on. As much as I'd like to stay this way with you forever, we have to get back. Rosa will have dinner ready and you're cold."

Stacy nodded and got up. She got dressed, watching as he refastened his jeans.

"If you keep looking at me like that, we'll be late and Dad will send out a search party." He laughed at her blush and helped her finish dressing, running his hands over her breasts as he buttoned her shirt. When he had her completely dressed again, he lifted her into his arms. She automatically wrapped her legs around his waist as he held her tightly against him.

"Stay, Stacy. This is your home. I'll do whatever it takes to make you happy here."

Her heart melted. She traced his bottom lip with her finger. "Oh, Wolfe. I wish I could. Please don't ruin this. I can't talk about this right now."

Wolfe stared at her for several long seconds before nodding. "Okay, sweetheart. But this isn't over. We *will* talk about this. Soon."

Stacy nodded but she knew she had to leave before then. She breathed a sigh of relief when Wolfe dropped the subject and lifted her into the saddle.

Riding back to the ranch, neither spoke. Wolfe's gaze kept sliding to her, and she turned to smile at him. He didn't smile back. His eyes traced down the length of her and back again so intently possessive she quivered. Her breasts swelled, the nipples reaching out to him across the slight distance. His eyes flicked to them, and his lips twitched before he looked away again.

Happiness like she'd never known filled her until she remembered that she had no choice but to leave all this. When they arrived back at the ranch, several hands stood in the yard and two came over to take their horses.

Wolfe leaned close and kissed her deeply. "I'm going to go get cleaned up. I'll see you at dinner." He tapped her bottom lip playfully before walking away.

She smiled and nodded and started walking up to the house. When she got close, she saw Travis and Cash coming out, and she wanted to bolt. "Hi," Cash grinned at her. "Did you and Wolfe have a nice ride?"

Nodding, her face burned and she tried to look away. Travis gripped her chin between a thumb and forefinger and studied her face. "You look better than you did earlier. Not as tense."

Her face burned even hotter. Not knowing how to answer him, she nodded and started toward the house. She couldn't very well tell him that the reason she looked better was because his brother had just taken her virginity, could she? Especially when the sight of Travis and Cash in their work clothes had begun to get her all hot and bothered again. No, the best thing she could do would be to avoid all of them as much as possible.

Her breasts still burned from Wolfe's touch, her panties still wet from his lovemaking. Yet the sound of Travis and Cash's low voices sent fissions of awareness through her. It made her want them to touch her as Wolfe had. Guilt consumed her. She could only imagine what Rex and Rosa would think of her if they knew.

No, she had to leave as soon as she'd made arrangements to sell the ranch. And she could never see any of them ever again.

"Did you have a nice ride?" Rosa asked, smiling at her as she stirred her stew.

Stacy paused in the doorway and smiled at Rosa as sadness almost overwhelmed her. She missed Rosa, missed the talks they had, the way Rosa greeted everyone when they came in and always had the house smelling of home cooking. Her apartment in Great Falls had never been a real home. God, she missed this place. She wished for what might have been if she could have fallen in love with only one of them. "Yes, Rosa. The ride was wonderful. If you don't mind, I think I'm going to go soak in the tub and get ready for bed." She laughed and even to her own ears it sounded hollow. "I haven't ridden for awhile, and I'm going to be sore."

Rosa frowned. "But you haven't eaten dinner."

Stacy ignored Rosa's searching look. "I'm not hungry. I'd just like to soak and go to bed." She kissed the older woman's cheek, wiping off a spot of flour. "I promise to eat a big breakfast tomorrow to make up for it. Good night." She just wanted to get to her room before any of the others came in.

Chapter Two

After her bath, Stacy donned a plain cotton gown and lay down on the bed. She'd pulled out a book to read earlier, and she picked it up hoping that reading would make her tired enough to sleep. Exhausted after her crying jag, and Wolfe's lovemaking, she now sat here wide awake.

Remembering the feel of Wolfe's hands on her made her breasts tingle. Now that she knew what it felt like to have him inside her, she would have a hard time avoiding him while she remained here. The way he'd made love to her and cared for her afterward simply melted her. His body had taken hers to remarkable heights, giving her pleasure she'd never imagined. His eyes, his lips, his tender touch made her feel desired and adored. He'd filled her body and her heart so completely, and it was a memory she'd always cherish.

She loved him so much and the way he had taken her had been so overwhelming and so complete, that she knew he would always have a part of her, always be a part of her. Thinking about the way her life would be without him in it nearly broke her. Before she'd always known that he and the others would be here. Now she didn't know where they would end up.

Would Wolfe be willing to leave his brothers to come back to Great Falls with her? Maybe if she told him the way she felt about him, he would. He had to feel something for her to say that he had waited for her for years.

Feeling better she drifted off to sleep, smiling as she remembered the look on Wolfe's face as he'd taken her virginity.

* * * *

The next morning she went downstairs, hugging Rosa from behind and kissing her. "Good morning!"

"Well good morning to you, too. You're certainly in a good mood this morning."

Stacy briefly thought about asking Rosa to come and join her in Great Falls. Rosa probably wouldn't go. She would never willingly leave Rex, but she would ask anyway. It would be better though, to wait until she had made some definite plans.

The first thing she had to do was to call her father's attorney. She had to settle the estate quickly so that she could put the ranch up for sale. She called the attorney's office and asked to speak with him.

"Of course, oh, may I ask who's calling, please?"

"This is Stacy Daniels. I'm calling about my father's estate."

"Oh, Ms. Daniels, I'm sorry. Mr. Freestone is out of the office. I'll leave him a message that you called."

"Thank you." That had been a little strange. She'd sounded like he was there at first. Shrugging, Stacy headed out in search of Wolfe.

As soon as she walked outside, she saw Rex standing at the fence, watching the horses. She walked up to him, bracing her arms on the top rail. "Hi, Rex."

Rex had been her father's foreman since Stacy was only ten years old. Her father had hated that the men listened to Rex more than to him but he couldn't fire him. He'd needed Rex to keep cowboys on the payroll. They usually quit after dealing with Benton.

"Hello, honey. How are you today?"

"I'm good." She frowned. "That makes me an awful person, doesn't it? The day after my father's funeral, and I'm happier than I've been in a long time."

"Your father was a bully, and you couldn't be an awful person if you tried."

If Rex only knew.

Her good mood deflated like a party balloon the day after, and she thought again about her options. If Wolfe wanted to stay at the ranch, could she stay, too? No. Not while Travis and Cash lived here. And she couldn't very well ask Travis and Cash to leave, could she? But if they stayed, her feelings for them would eventually show and then what would happen? Fights. Hurt feelings.

No, she couldn't do that to any of them. They didn't deserve it. Just because she was selfish didn't mean that she had to hurt the people she loved. Damn. She wished she could ask Rosa or Rex what to do. They'd always been there for all of her problems but she just couldn't ask them about this.

Maybe she just needed to get away from all of them for a little while. Just to think. She couldn't keep hiding her emotions, and she needed some time alone. That's what she'd do. She'd just go away for a couple of days. Maybe by then she would be able to talk to her father's attorney and get the estate settled.

"Something on your mind?"

She shuffled her feet. Rex and Rosa always knew when something bothered her. It reinforced her decision. "I was thinking about going away for a couple of days."

"Why?"

Surprised, she looked up at him. "Well, to think."

"Don't see why you have to go away to do that. There's plenty of thinking room right here."

Stacy couldn't prevent a smile at Rex's answer. He always whittled things to the simplest terms and as far as she knew, had never been wrong. But she needed this. "I need to get away from everybody for a while. I need to be alone."

Rex didn't speak for several moments and just when she thought he wouldn't, he said softly. "You know that my sons all love you, don't you?"

"Yes." She smiled sadly. She knew that Rex thought his sons all loved her like a little sister. "I love them, too." That had always been the problem.

When she told Rosa of her decision to go away for a few days, the older woman didn't like it at all.

"Why do you have to go away? Your father's not here anymore."

"I just want some time alone, Rosa. I have some thinking to do."

"There's plenty of thinking room here at the ranch."

Stacy smiled at how alike Rosa and Rex sounded. "I know but I just have to get away for a couple of days. I have my cell phone if you need to call me."

Rosa continued to grumble as Stacy went to her room to pack. She just took a couple of day's worth of clothing, throwing in a dress in case she got an appointment with the attorney. Saying goodbye to a still grumbling Rosa, she left.

She drove into the next town and almost stopped before she thought better of it. She didn't actually want to hide but she didn't want to be found either. She just wanted some time alone, and she didn't want to run into anyone she knew. Stopping for a burger, she went past a cheap motel to one that looked a little better. It didn't look exactly high dollar but being a woman alone, she didn't want to take any chances. She could just imagine what kind of trouble she'd be in when she got home if something had happened.

Checking in, she asked for a room near the back so that her car couldn't be seen from the road. After getting into the room, she decided that a shower would relax her. She'd bought a few magazines to read and a book if she had trouble falling asleep.

The hot shower made her feel better, and she threw a robe on, not wanting to bother with a nightgown. She'd never slept nude before, but thinking about her time with Wolfe made her body hot. Even though the air outside had cooled, she kept the windows closed and turned on the air conditioner.

Lying in bed with her magazines, she remembered how good it had been when Wolfe touched her nipples. She reached up to touch them, frustrated that she couldn't get the same feeling on her own. Feeling the moisture between her legs, she slid a finger through her folds. It didn't feel the same as Wolfe's fingers. She wanted to howl in frustration.

When her cell phone rang, she jumped and nearly fell off the bed. Looking at the display, she groaned. It was the ranch phone. She knew she had to answer in case it was an emergency. Damn.

"Hello?"

"What do you think you're doing?"

Stacy shuddered at the deep timber of Cash's voice. "What do you mean?"

"Don't play games with me, Stacy. You're going to lose."

"Didn't Rosa and Rex tell all of you that I went away for a few days?"

"Yes. Why?"

Stacy snapped. "I just want some time alone to think, okay?"

"Watch your tone."

Stacy's eyes widened at the moisture that dripped from her now at Cash's dark tone. He'd never spoken that way to her before. She put a hand to her stomach and took a deep breath. "I just want to be alone, okay?"

"No, it's not okay. We're all worried. Anything could happen to you. Where are you?"

"Listen, I'll be home in a couple of days. Don't call me again unless it's an emergency." She disconnected before he could reply. Her stomach clenched. She would be in big trouble now. Cash would be hurt that she'd hung up on him, and Wolfe might be upset that she'd left. She already knew that Rex and Rosa had thought going away had been a stupid idea. Why couldn't they just let her have some time alone?"

Nervous now, she tightened the belt of the robe and moved to the window to look out. Seeing no one she knew, she laughed at herself. Of course they didn't know where she was.

Picking up the magazine, she started reading again and came to an article about what men wanted in a woman. The men interviewed had answered so predictably that it surprised her that the magazine had even wasted the space to print it. Nice smiles and good personalities. Please. That's why men stampeded over everyone in their path when they saw a woman with bleached blonde hair and big breasts, because they liked her smile.

Lying on her stomach, she continued to read the magazine, lost in an article about foods popular in different parts of the country. Rosa would like this, and she continued to read.

She had no warning. Someone using a keycard opened her door, and she bolted. Before she could take two steps, she'd been grabbed from behind, her arms held behind her back. Oh my God! She whimpered, scared to death, kicking out furiously when a voice sounded next to her ear.

"What would you have done if it had been a stranger?"

"Cash. You son of a bitch! You scared me to death."

He let her go and closed the door. "You didn't even have the deadbolt locked."

He grabbed her again from behind, wrapping his arms around her and pulling her back against him. His deep voice rumbled against her neck. "Thank God you're okay. If anyone else had come through that door-"

"I would have locked it before I went to bed." If she told him she'd forgotten all about it she didn't know what he would do. His hands moved up to cup her breasts and she dropped her head on his shoulder. Having him wrapped around her this way sizzled her senses. Her breasts swelled. Her nipples hardened against his palms. Damn it. Why couldn't she resist him? Her robe had come undone in their struggle. She pulled away and quickly tightened it. She walked to the chair and sat down, not wanting to risk sitting back on the bed.

She pushed back her still damp hair and stared at him. "What are you doing here? I told all of you that I want to be alone. How did you find me?"

Cash studied her for several seconds, and she forced herself not to squirm. "I'm not going to tell you. You never know when it may come in handy again."

"Don't tell me then. I don't care. You see that I'm fine. Goodbye."

Cash shook his head. "I'm not leaving. If you're going to spend the night here, then so am I. Tomorrow morning we'll go back to the ranch."

"You can't sleep in this room. Go get another room. I'll see you tomorrow." She'd wait until he got another room and then she'd move to another hotel. Amazing. Now that her father could no longer run her life, Wolfe and Cash thought they could.

"No."

"What do you mean no?"

"N-O. No. I'm not leaving and neither are you, until tomorrow morning. We're going to sleep right here. First, though, I'm going to paddle your ass for taking off the way you did *and* for hanging up on me *and* for not locking the damned door. You scared the hell out of all of us by leaving."

Stacy blinked at the surge of pure lust that went through her. He couldn't be serious. And what the hell was wrong with her? "What did you say?"

Cash leaned down and lifted her chin, capturing her lips in a kiss so blatantly sexual, she had no choice but to respond. He parted her robe as he continued to kiss her and she gasped into his mouth at the feel of his hands on her breasts. It felt different than when Wolfe had touched her there but just as good. Why couldn't she make them feel that way herself?

He lifted her from the chair, and she went willingly, wrapping her arms around his waist as he held her closely. Running her hands over his back, she reveled in the muscles she found there, feeling small and vulnerable in his arms. The feeling escalated when he pushed her robe from her shoulders, allowing it to puddle at her feet.

Now totally naked, the rough denim brushed against her thighs and his shirt chafed her nipples. Deliberately, she rubbed them across the soft cotton over and over, loving the friction on them. He pulled her arms from around his waist and put them at her sides.

He put his hands on her waist, and she leaned into him, crying out as he pulled her against him and took several steps toward the bed. She tried to hang on but before she knew it she'd been flipped over his lap and staring down at the ugly hotel carpet. Struggling uselessly, she cried out. "What are you doing?"

He positioned her the way he wanted despite her struggles and pressed a hard hand at the small of her back.

"Let me go, you bastard!" The feel of his hand coming down hard on her bottom surprised her so much that she stilled for a moment. Then she began struggling in earnest.

He stroked a hand over her warm bottom. "Damn it. I can't." He picked her up and cradled her on his lap, holding her tightly against him. "I can't even spank you. You scared me to death, baby."

Amazed at the shudder that went through him, she lifted her arms around his neck and held him tightly. He'd sent her into a tailspin. The angry slap on her bottom followed by his tenderness and the almost desperate way he held her confused and warmed her at the same time.

His hands continued to caress her back as he buried his face in her neck. "Why did you run away, baby?"

"I'm a grown woman. I didn't run away. I just wanted to be alone."

He lifted his face and smiled at her so tenderly, it brought tears to her eyes. "Your days of being alone are over, sweetheart. The sooner you get used to that, the better."

He caressed her back, and she arched, moaning deep in her throat as his hands slid over her. She heard his chuckle and tensed.

"No, don't tense up on me. You're so soft, honey. Stroking you is like stroking a soft, sleek, cat. You even purr. Let me see if I can make you purr some more."

"Let me go." She responded to him as strongly as she had to Wolfe. This couldn't be good.

"Never. Spread your legs for me."

His hands moved to caress her thighs, and she froze. Only Wolfe had ever touched her there. She couldn't allow this. Struggling again in earnest now, Stacy fought like a wildcat, scared of these new sensations running through her body.

Her breasts just throbbed, and she wanted to touch them but she wouldn't be able to until Cash had gone. An unbelievable amount of moisture dripped from her. She wondered if Cash could feel it.

He kept her in place easily, shifting her slightly. He stroked her thighs again, distracting her, before lifting her one handed to undo his jeans. Oh my God. What would she do? He sat back down with her on his lap.

The hair on his bare thighs tickled her own. His hard cock pushed at her as his caresses continued.

"Do you have any idea just how long I've wanted you?"

Stacy blinked. "You have?"

The tender smile he gave her made her stomach clench. His hands moved over her breasts and she looked down, watching in fascination as a callused finger traced lightly over a nipple. The throbbing of her clit matched the strokes of his finger. When his other hand moved over her hip, she moaned, gripping him tightly.

She wanted him so much she couldn't stand it. Her body was on fire, the heat between her legs burning her. It got even worse when he gripped a nipple between a thumb and forefinger and allowed her own movement to give her even more pleasure. She would die of it.

"Open your legs for me, Stacy. Let me know if you want me."

She had no choice but to obey him, never even made the conscious effort to do so. Her body responded to his words while her mind turned to mush. She opened her thighs for him, needing him to see how much she wanted him. She needed his hands on her, needed to feel him inside her.

She held her breath as his hand slid from her breast and moved between her thighs, sliding over her mound, and froze when he circled her opening.

"Are you afraid?"

"N-no."

"Good girl. Let me feel your wet little pussy."

His rough fingers slid through her folds, and she jolted at the sensation as a fresh rush of moisture escaped.

"You're almost ready to come, honey." He moved his fingers away from her clit, and she arched, trying to follow.

He chuckled again. "No, honey. No coming for you. You've been a bad girl."

"Please, Cash. I can't stand it."

He shifted her position, pulling her until her head became even with his thighs. His cock brushed against her cheek. Fisting his hand in her hair, he pulled it aside and turned her face so that he could see her. "Take my cock in that hot little mouth of your and suck it. I'm dying to feel your mouth on me, honey. I've waited a long time for it. Let me feel it, please, honey."

Stacy had never done this before but she'd read about it in her magazines. She eagerly turned her face and took him in her mouth, trying to remember everything she'd ever read. His finger pressed inside her dripping pussy which made thinking impossible so she gave into her hunger for him and sucked him as deeply as she could. Running her tongue over him made him hiss.

The thought that she finally had him this way, alone and practically naked, made her hotter. She sucked him as hard as she could, taking him to the back of her throat. He released her hair to pinch her nipple, and she moaned at the wonderful jolt of lust that made her tighten on his finger. She'd loved him for so long, wanted him for so long, and couldn't resist this chance to be with him. It might very well be the only one she'd ever get.

Pushing all other thoughts from her mind, she concentrated only on Cash.

She thrust herself on his thick finger over and over, the action also thrusting his cock into her mouth. The sudden warning tingling she'd felt with Wolfe started. Just when she thought she would find her pleasure, he withdrew from her.

"No coming yet. You're so beautiful, Stacy, so responsive." His harsh groans sounded wonderful. The more she could wring groans from him, the hotter she got. His rough voice got lower. His hands tightened on her hair. "I'm going to come. Honey. If you don't want me to come in your mouth, you have to stop, honey."

She answered by gripping his thighs tighter. She wanted, *needed*, all of him.

His muscles tightened as he spurted into her mouth. "Fuck."

She swallowed over and over, even more aroused that she had brought him this kind of pleasure. His harsh groans made her feel powerful and desired. She continued to lick him while he stroked her hair and face.

"That's it, honey. Lick me clean, little cat. God, you're incredible."

She loved the feel of him on her tongue, loved his erotic taste. When she had finished, he pulled her head away and lifted her, curling her into his arms and taking her mouth with his. His kiss tormented her, not thrusting his tongue into her mouth, but teasing her until she chased him. He played with her over and over until finally she grabbed his hair and pulled him forcefully against her.

He chuckled and gave her what she wanted, laying her on the bed and pressing her into the mattress. He took her mouth boldly, hardly allowing her to breathe. Lifting his head, he looked down at her and she couldn't help but lift up to him in offering. Smiling wickedly, he ran his hand down her body before standing to refasten his jeans.

He moved to the foot of the bed, staring at her. Her breasts throbbed so much she reached up to touch them, past caring if he saw her.

He grinned. "Do your breasts need to be stroked, honey?"

"Open your legs wide for me, little cat."

Stacy looked down and thrilled at the big muscular man, seemingly enthralled by the sight of her pussy. She needed him desperately and would gladly do whatever he wanted if he would just end this torment. She opened her legs for him, lifting again for his touch. So aroused, she shook. She didn't know how much more of this she could take.

His smile as he moved between her legs made her shudder. With rough hands grabbing the backs of knees, he lifted them high and wide.

The cool air from the air conditioner breathed over her soaked folds, and she gripped the pillow tightly in her hands and lifted even more. Desire like she'd never known raced through her, and her moans and whimpers filled the room.

"I've wanted to taste you forever. I've wanted my mouth on you for years, little cat."

"Oh God." The first touch of his tongue on her slit had her crying out at the too sharp sensation. Wrapped in a blanket of lust, nothing existed for her except the heated friction that traced her folds over and over again. His hands moved up her body to cover her breasts, his fingers tugging lightly at her nipples.

When he pushed his tongue into her heat, she arched, crying out as he stabbed her again and again. Thrashing on the pillow against the unfamiliar feel, she tightened her hands on the bedding as she started to spin out of control. He moved his mouth to her clit, closing his lips over it and she froze as he sucked it into his mouth, and her entire body sizzled.

The pleasure that washed over her touched every part of her body, tingles of delight racing everywhere. She cried out at the indescribable feel of sublime ecstasy that spread from her core and exploded throughout her. He licked the cream from her, cleaning her the way she had cleaned him, and the feel of his tongue on her too-tender flesh made her tremble even more.

His mouth moved up to her stomach, placing opened mouth kisses all over her and moving higher. He used the flat of his tongue on her sensitive nipples before lifting to again take her mouth with his. She opened to him readily for whatever he wanted, tasting herself on his tongue as he possessed her mouth with his.

He lifted his head but she couldn't open her eyes to meet his. They'd become too heavy, her body replete and exhausted. He lifted, then shifted her, and she settled against him, trusting his strength. He pulled down the bedding and laid her on the cool sheets. She had almost fallen asleep when he touched his lips to her forehead.

"I've waited forever for you, kitten. You won't be able to run far enough to get away from me now."

Chapter Three

Stacy looked in the rearview mirror again, seeing Cash's big truck right on her tail. They hadn't even stopped to eat breakfast before he plucked her out of bed, told her to get dressed and went outside to wait in his truck for her to follow her home.

So much for her few days alone.

This morning he looked even more menacing. She could hear the scratching sound as he ran a hand over his whiskers. "If I didn't have these, I'd lap more of my kitten's cream. Your pussy is too soft for these, so let's get going. Wolfe and Travis are waiting for us."

He'd walked out of the room, and she'd slunk to the bed, wondering what the hell she was going to do. If Wolfe found out what had happened last night—

She thought about it the whole ride back, and the closer they got to the ranch, the more her stomach clenched in fear. She had to get in touch with the attorney. As soon as she put the ranch up for sale, she would leave.

Riding through town, she saw with relief that the attorney's office had cars parked out front. He had to be in. As soon as they pulled up to the ranch, Stacy grabbed her bag and raced into the house, not waiting for Cash. Feeling guilty about what she'd done to Wolfe, she just couldn't face him right now.

She ran up to her bedroom and stripped, jumping into the shower. The heated water running over her body reminded her too much of Cash's hands running over it the night before so she showered quickly. Rubbing her skin briskly with the towel as though punishing herself for her stupidity and weakness that made her vulnerable to both Wolfe and Cash, she dried off and got dressed.

Rosa came in as she worked the tangles out of her hair and a thought occurred to her. "Rosa, would you do me a favor and call the attorney for me? He's never there."

She had called several times and thought it strange that he hadn't gotten back to her yet. It was almost like he wanted to avoid her. Rosa looked at her strangely, probably wondering why she just didn't call herself, but Stacy slid her eyes away and pulled her wet hair into a ponytail.

When Rosa hung up the phone, she turned to Stacy. "He's in." She frowned. "Stacy, Mr. Freestone is in his office every day. Are you sure you called the right number?"

Suspicious now, she nevertheless smiled at Rosa. "No. I probably called the wrong number. Thanks, Rosa."

Rosa went to her suitcase and pulled out the dirty clothes. "So much for your getting away, huh? Those boys were not at all happy to find out you'd gone."

Stacy turned to look at her, her stomach filling with dread. "Did Wolfe know that I was gone?"

Rosa looked at her incredulously. "Of course he knew. Wolfe knows everything that happens on the ranch."

Stacy gulped. "What did he say?"

Rosa walked over to Stacy and hugged her, their eyes meeting in the mirror. "You know Wolfe. He says more not saying anything than most people do when they're running their mouths. He just got this real hard look on his face and didn't say anything for a couple of minutes. Then he looked at Cash and said, 'Go get her'."

Stacy gulped and looked away, no longer being able to face Rosa. "Did he seem really mad?"

Rosa looked uncomfortable as she moved around Stacy's bedroom, straightening things that didn't need to be straightened.

"Don't you worry about him. You could always wrap all of the Dakota men around your little finger."

"So he was mad."

"He got that cold look, you know the one that can freeze a person on the spot? Then he got a really strange look on his face and got up from the table and left."

"I wonder why he didn't come get me himself," Stacy murmured.

"Probably too busy, although he always has time for you." Rosa frowned then shook her head as though clearing it. "Maybe he was just too mad. I don't know. What I do know is that if I don't get busy, lunch will be late, and I'll have four hungry, angry men in my kitchen."

Stacy went down a few minutes later and got herself a glass of juice and a piece of toast. "Rosa, I'm going to go into town and talk to Mr. Freestone. I'll grab something in town for lunch."

She met Rosa's worried look. "Don't worry. I'm not going anywhere. Just into town. I wouldn't take off without telling you."

* * * *

Mr. Freestone's secretary looked startled to see her, really startled. "Mr. Freestone is very busy this afternoon, Ms. Daniels. Perhaps you'd like to make an appointment."

Stacy stood with her hands on her hips and frowned at the woman. "I tried that. He won't even return my calls. What the hell is going on? I need to settle my father's estate."

Hearing loud voices, the attorney came out, blanching when he saw Stacy. What the hell? "Ms. Daniels. I really don't have time for you today. Maybe one day next week."

Enraged that they'd lied to her, Stacy went toe-to-toe with the attorney, and he turned even whiter. "I want to settle my father's estate. You'd better make time for me right now!" Peering past him, she saw that no one sat in his office. "It looks like you're free. This shouldn't take too long."

She walked past him into his office and sat in a chair, waiting for him to join her. "Just give me whatever I have to sign so I can have the deed to the ranch."

"What are you doing to do with it?"

"That really isn't your concern, now, is it?" she asked sarcastically. "Just show me what I need to sign."

Stacy noticed with some surprise that Mr. Freestone kept wiping his face with his handkerchief. She could see the perspiration on his forehead and upper lip. Something had to be very wrong. A lead weight settled in the pit of her stomach. She'd try the soft approach. "Mr. Freestone," she began softly. "I just want to get all of this out of the way so that I can get back to my life. Please help me."

He brightened somewhat, which threw her. "Oh, you want to get back to Great Falls. Don't worry then, dear. There's nothing for you to worry about. Your father sold everything to Wolfe, Travis and Cash Dakota. You're free of the ranch. It isn't your problem anymore."

* * * *

Stacy walked out of the attorney's office, and down the street and somehow ended up at the park, not even remembering how she'd gotten there. Her father had hated her so much that he hadn't even told her that he'd sold the ranch. Why had he sold it? So she would never have it?

She'd always thought that one day the ranch would be hers. She loved her home, and she loved the people on it. To come to grips with the fact that her father had hated her so much that he would even take the ranch from her was more than she thought she could bear. A strange numbness settled over her. She sat there too hurt to cry, too stunned to absorb it. He'd given her in death what he'd given her in life. Pain. Heartache. Even though she had planned to sell it, he wouldn't have known that. He'd had no qualms about selling her home and not even telling her.

Why had she never been able to get used to it? Why had she continued to hope that he would have seen something in her to love?

Tears rolled down her face. Her face had become soaked with them, but she couldn't sob or yell or rage at her father's hatred. It stunned her so much, filled her with such grief that she could do nothing but sit there while the tears flowed. The trees and the children playing all around blurred. She gripped the bench tightly, feeling that if she let go she would fall.

She had no idea how long she sat there before she felt a presence at her side. She didn't even have the will to fight when she was lifted onto hard thighs and held against a hot muscular chest. Wolfe.

She would know his scent anywhere. He didn't speak, just held her, and the sobs began. She cried so hard she had trouble breathing and her throat hurt as he silently rocked her in his arms. She cried forever and when her sobs had been reduced to hiccups, he tilted her face up to wipe her tears.

Looking up into his face, she saw the tender expression she knew was reserved just for her. Suddenly the overwhelming guilt, thinking over her lovemaking with Cash threatened to crush her. She didn't deserve him. Still not speaking, he touched his lips softly to hers and lifted her as though she weighed nothing, walking across the park with her in his arms. When he got to his truck, he put her in without a word, holding her hand in his all the way back to the ranch.

When they pulled in, Rosa, Rex, Travis and Cash came outside. Wolfe waved them back and came around for her, lifting her into his arms again and carrying her into the house. She hid her face in his neck, not wanting to face anyone.

"Is she alright?" She heard Rosa ask.

For the first time, Wolfe spoke. "She'll be fine now. She's home."

* * * *

Stacy stayed in her room the rest of the day, thinking about what she'd learned. Why had her father sold the ranch to them? Had it only been to make sure that she never got it? *When* had he sold it to them? Had it been only recently or had they owned the ranch for years?

Had she been coming to visit a place that hadn't even belonged to them?

If they owned the ranch, why had none of them moved inside? Only her father and Rosa had lived in the house, her father upstairs in the master bedroom and Rosa in her apartment off the kitchen.

Her room had never been changed, and she always stayed there when she visited. How come nobody told her that it didn't belong to her any more? Every time she came home, her things remained just as she'd left them. Her hat and boots never even got moved. Even her father had never gotten rid of anything of hers. Why?

Why hadn't her father told her? She would have thought her father would have gotten a lot of satisfaction out of telling her that the ranch would never be hers.

She had too many questions, and they had started to give her a headache.

She heard the men come in and looked at her clock. Dinnertime. She went downstairs to help Rosa, avoiding the men's searching looks as she helped Rosa put the food on the table. Rex joined them as usual, he and Wolfe mostly just listening to the conversation going on around them.

She didn't speak, not trusting herself not to cry. She ate silently, listening to Rosa talk with Travis and Cash about their day and trivial things, and she had the impression that they kept the conversation light for her benefit.

Finally she couldn't stand it any more. "How long have you owned the ranch?" she asked quietly. All conversation ended. She looked up to find everyone looking at Wolfe.

He took his time, finishing the food in his mouth before answering. "Five years."

Stacy felt all the blood drain from her face. "I left five years ago."

Wolfe nodded and continued eating.

Frustrated by his silence, she looked at Cash. "If you bought this place five years ago, why did my father still live here?"

"It was one of the terms of the sale."

"Why didn't he tell me?"

"Same answer."

When Travis glared at him, he glared back. "Then you answer her questions!"

"Why didn't you ever eat in the kitchen before? Why didn't you move into the house?"

Cash shoved food in his mouth and raised a brow at Travis. Travis looked at her and sighed. "We couldn't stand your father. We didn't want to live with him and didn't want to eat with him."

"Why did he sell?" She looked from one to the other and wondered if anyone would answer. Finally Cash did. "He ran the place into the ground. He was broke. He couldn't even afford to keep the hands."

Stacy rubbed her head. Her headache had started to get worse. Getting information out of them was like pulling teeth. She looked at Rosa. "You knew about this, didn't you? You knew even when you called the attorney for me."

When several pairs of eyes looked at Rosa accusingly, Stacy hurriedly added, "I'd been trying to call and got suspicious when his secretary kept putting me off."

Rosa got up for more iced tea and patted her shoulder. "You don't have to defend me. I never liked that they kept it from you. I thought you had a right to know but they wouldn't let me tell you. Now you know, and you don't have to worry about it anymore. They'll all take care of everything."

Stacy remembered what they'd said earlier. She looked at Wolfe, wanting the answer from him. "Why did you make my dad stay? Why did you make it a condition of the sale?"

She waited impatiently as he watched her intently before answering. "So you would keep coming back."

Stacy started laughing, and when she started, she found she couldn't stop. She laughed until her sides hurt, laughed until she started shaking with sobs, becoming hysterical, and she still couldn't stop. Big tears rolled down her face. Rosa pulled her close, and she cried against her chest, her arms around Rosa's waist.

When she'd settled some, she wrenched herself away from Rosa and stood. She looked at each of them to find them all staring at her in concern. "I didn't come here to see my father. I came to see all of you. And all this time you lied to me. I came back here because I love all of you so much and now I've ruined even that. I've got nothing left anymore. I certainly no longer have a reason to stay."

She spun and left the room, running up to her bedroom and slamming the door. No. Not her bedroom. Nothing here belonged to her anymore. The men had always showed her nothing but love and look what she'd done. She'd already betrayed Wolfe, and she just couldn't live with that. She paced her room for a long time, not able to settle down. She heard the men leave when they'd finished eating. Still she paced. Once it got dark she thought about going back downstairs. Hearing murmured voices coming from that direction, she decided against it.

Knowing she'd been a fool all these years, she didn't want to face them again. She knew they would hear her if she went down the stairs, so she climbed out the window of her room. She'd done it a hundred times before, shimmying down the slanted roof, dropping down on the railing of the back porch to freedom.

She'd done many times what she did now, whenever she needed to get away from some hurt that her father had inflicted. She ran for the stables with the intent of saddling one of the horses and riding.

Wolfe would be mad if he knew. She wasn't allowed to ride alone or at night, but she wouldn't be gone long, and he wouldn't find out.

When she ran into the stable, the door behind her slammed shut, and the bolt clicked in place. She spun, wondering who could be out here. The large figure moved slowly into the light until she finally saw his face, but once he'd moved, she'd already recognized him.

Travis.

"Off on one of your pouts?"

"I don't pout."

"Couldn't have proved it by me."

Stacy shuffled her feet. "I just wanted to go for a ride."

"Are you allowed to ride by yourself?"

Stacy found herself taking a step back for every one he took forward. She raised her chin defiantly, not wanting him to know that he scared her. Travis was not a man to be trifled with. "No."

"Are you allowed to ride at night?"

"No."

"Seems to me you've been breaking a lot of rules in a short amount of time."

Not knowing how to respond to that, Stacy remained silent.

"Wolfe and I made rules for you for your own protection. We've let you get away with a lot over the years because your daddy tried to bully you. He's gone now, and you're our responsibility."

Stacy bristled at that. "I'm not your responsibility. Since the ranch is no longer mine to worry about I'm leaving."

She's known Travis most of her life. She'd seen him pound other men to dust, seen his eyes flare with hot temper, seen him strike hard and fast many times over the years. But she'd never before had it directed at her.

The brief flash of temper in his eyes froze her in fear. He'd looked like a man in a rage. Travis in a rage had to be the second most terrifying thing she could imagine. Wolfe's icy temper would be, hands down, the first.

He moved closer, stalking her. His long legs ate up the distance quickly. Before she could bolt, he had her. Lightning fast, he bent a shoulder to her stomach, gripped her thighs and straightened, all in one move. Just like that she found herself over his shoulder.

He climbed to the loft over the stable, and she closed her eyes against the terrifying height. She didn't dare squirm, afraid she would knock him off balance and both of them would take a nasty tumble.

The hand on her thighs held her firmly and created an unwelcome warmth between her legs. Lord help her. Why did she have to have these feelings with all *three* of them?

She should have known Travis would have no trouble carrying her. When he got to the top, he dropped her into a pile of straw, glaring down at her. The window high on the side wall allowed the silver light from the almost full moon to come through. Her breath caught in her throat as Travis moved, and the light caught his face. The harsh shadows made him look even more powerful and unforgiving.

The Travis she'd always dealt with had been indulgent and tender. He and Wolfe had been the ones to lay down the rules, firmly but with gentle consideration of her feelings. She didn't know how to deal with this Travis.

"So you're not our responsibility, and you don't want to obey the rules that have been laid down for you? And you threaten to leave."

"Travis, you have to listen to me."

"Oh, do I? I think it's a better idea to get you to listen to me."

He lunged for her, and she had no chance of escaping him. He took her down, landing on her hard, not as hard as she knew he could have, even now trying to protect her by holding most of his weight of off her. Grabbing her head in his hands, he tilted her mouth to his and ravaged her. There was no other word for it. He took her mouth over and over, eating at her as though starved for the taste of her.

The response he drew from her came immediately and completely. She couldn't deny him any of it. The delicious feel of so much hard packed muscle surrounding her heated her blood. She'd loved him for so long that the feel of finally having him around her, holding her closely against him, made her hold on tight and grab desperately for more.

He kissed her hotly, his mouth unyielding. His hands moved to her waist, gathered her t-shirt and lifted from her only long enough to rip it over her head. He forced her thighs apart with one of his and moved between them. His mouth moved to her neck as her bra came undone. She cried out at the feel of his hot mouth and firm hands on her breasts. Her entire body shook with the pleasure he gave her.

There was nothing subtle about Travis. He moved fast and hard, taking what he wanted, and she found herself climbing so hot and so high that a little place in the back of her mind almost feared it. He stripped her of all control, all defenses in a heartbeat and took her where he wanted her to be.

His mouth at her breast licked and sucked and nipped at her, making her writhe with need. The pull on her nipples went straight to her slit and already her panties had become soaked. He unfastened her jeans and with a last nip at her nipple, he leaned back.

The last nip had made her nipple sting, and she couldn't believe the jolt of pleasure that went through her. He rolled her to her side and jerked her jeans and her panties down her legs.

She heard him curse as they tangled on her sneakers, and he pulled them and her socks off before ridding her of her jeans and panties. Quivering with need, she now lay before him completely naked. An overlying sense of rightness filled her. Even in his present mood, he wrapped a warm blanket of security all around her. Nothing could ever hurt her when she had one of them around.

He stared down at her body for several moments before finally reaching out to touch her. Caught in the sliver of moonlight, his face looked harder than she had ever seen it before, and she shivered even as more moisture coated her thighs.

He leaned over her, caging her in with his big body. He watched his own hand as it moved over her breasts, plucking at her nipples. She scarcely breathed when his hand moved over her stomach and over the curls on her mound. Pushing a hand between her thighs, he separated her folds with his fingers.

"Do you have any idea how long I've waited for you? Do you know what just being around you does to me? Do you know how many times I wanted to kill your father for the way he treated you?"

Stunned to her toes, Stacy lifted her eyes to his. They blazed as they held hers. His expression looked fierce as he rubbed his chest against her nipples while stroking softly over her folds.

Stacy arched and gasped when a thick finger pressed into her and a thumb touched her clit. When he spoke, his words came through gritted teeth. "This is your home. You will stay here where you belong. After tonight you'll know better than to threaten me with leaving, and you'll know better than to break the rules we made to keep you safe."

Stacy didn't have any time to respond before he'd picked her up with one hand, dangling her over his arm as he pulled a bale of hay closer with the other. Sitting down on the hay, he flipped her over his lap. She knew that he could see her bare bottom in the moonlight and she tried to pull away.

"Please, Travis, don't do this."

"It's too late for that. Next time you'll think about the consequences of threatening me or with disobeying your rules."

With that he began to slap her bottom. She fought, and she cried out as he paddled both her cheeks over and over until they started to burn. Embarrassed by the flood of moisture on her thighs, she kept them closed tightly. His slaps became less frequent and less intense until they'd become caresses.

"Damn it." He flipped her into his lap, his face at her neck, his arms tight bands of steel around her. "Christ, baby. I'm sorry. I'm so sorry. You make me crazy when you threaten to leave. Stay, baby.

Please." He lifted his head. "You love the ranch. Don't threaten to leave again. Follow the rules. We just want to keep you safe. God, I don't know what I'd do if anything happened to you."

He kissed her almost desperately, his hand sliding over her stomach and back down to her folds. He lifted his head and smiled at her. "You liked your spanking, didn't you, you little hellcat?"

"No. You hurt my bottom."

His chuckle sounded darkly erotic. "Your soft little pussy is dripping."

His eyes appeared lit from within. "I'm going to take you in the most intimate way a man can take a woman. I'll make it good for you, baby. I need you so damned much." He moved his mouth over her lingeringly before straightening. His hands were gentle as he flipped her to her stomach.

She moaned when his hands moved over her back and bottom. The hand on her bottom burned her heated skin.

"You have the cutest little butt." He held one cheek in each of his hands, his thumbs moving toward her crease.

Stacy gasped when he separated them and slid thick fingers through her folds. "Oh, please Travis, do something."

"Oh, I'm going to do something alright. Just not what you had planned." His eyes searched hers. "Do you trust me, baby? Will you trust me to take care of you, to not hurt you?"

Surrounded by Travis' heat and strength, his desire for her plain to see, she could do nothing but surrender. She needed to give herself to him and she wanted to take all that he offered. Her body and her heart cried out for him. She turned to look up at him. "Yes. I want you so much. I trust you completely. Please, Travis. Take me."

His smiled flashed before he looked down her body again. "Look at this pretty little rosebud."

His fingers, slick with her own juices, slid up over and over to touch her forbidden opening. She grabbed onto his leg desperately as circled her opening with his finger. She gasped and cried out when he began to press into her anus.

"You're very tight here, baby. I'm going to have to stretch you a bit."

"Oh God." She tried to buck as he pushed his finger into her but nothing she did or said could sway him. "It burns." She stopped squirming when it only moved her on his finger.

"Relax, baby. Breathe deeply for me. Jesus, you have the tightest ass."

She'd never thought of having anything in her bottom before. It felt forbidden and naughty, and she thought she just might die of it. She would give him anything. She would give him her soul if she could. Parting her thighs even more, she arched further onto his finger.

"You're so perfect for me, baby. You're pushing onto my finger. You like having something in your ass, don't you? Let's see how much your tight little bottom likes having two fingers inside it."

A chill went down her spine. How much more of this could she stand? When he slid his finger from her and gathered more moisture, she held her breath and then groaned as two thick fingers pushed their way inside her. Oh. It felt so darkly erotic to be touched this way, so forbidden. Her juices dripped from her, running down her thighs and probably onto his denim clad leg.

She began to push back in time with his strokes as he pushed more and more of his fingers into her. When he moved them around inside her anus, she arched, jolting at the extreme sensation.

"You like that. You like giving yourself this way. I love touching you this way. I can have it all baby, can't I? Let me see if I can make you want me as much as I've always wanted you."

Perspiration covered her body. She writhed and moaned as Travis pushed three fingers into her. She spread her legs wide, pushing up onto his fingers as they forged their way inside her. "It burns. Oh, Travis. It feels incredible."

He groaned. "God, honey. If you knew what seeing you this way does to me."

Stacy bucked and clawed at his leg, not knowing how to channel the feelings he brought about. Her body raged like an inferno, the place between her legs burned so hot while her juices continued to flow out of her. When he removed his fingers from her ass, she started whimpering, unable to stand the now empty feeling.

"Please Travis. Do something. Don't leave me like this. I need something. Please."

His hand rubbed over her bottom soothingly. "Easy, baby. I'll take care of you."

He lifted her from his lap, steadying her until she could stand alone. He whipped off his shirt and she reached for his chest hungrily. Strongly muscled, his dark chest shone with sweat, making it glow in the moonlight. He turned from her, and she saw that he had placed his shirt over the bale of hay he'd been sitting on.

He picked her up and laid her gently over it, positioning her to his satisfaction.

Stacy started to shake really badly, fear and excitement warring in her body. "W-what are you going to do to me?"

He leaned over her from behind, his naked body completely covering hers. His cock pressed against her and she closed her eyes as she got an idea of his size. The Dakota man were all big everywhere.

Travis moved close to her, his breath hot on her ear. "I'm going to slowly work my cock in that tight little ass of yours and fuck it until you scream with pleasure. You're never going to forget how good I can make you feel."

Travis lifted from her, running a hand down her back from her neck to her bottom. He spread her legs even further apart. Sliding a finger through her folds, he gathered more of her moisture.

"I don't need any lube with you, do I, darlin'? You have plenty of juice for me. One day soon I'm going to get my mouth on that pussy and feast. I'm going to eat you alive."

Stacy shook with the force of her arousal as Travis pressed more of her juices inside her anus. She held her breath on a whimper when he posed his cock at her entrance. Shuddering, she tightened her hands into fists as he pushed his hips forward, forging his way inside her.

She panted and cried out at the burning, the too intense feeling of her ass being invaded. She felt so small, so vulnerable at such a dominant act. In that moment he owned her. He could do what he would with her, and she lay bent over for him, completely open and a slave to his desires.

"Travis. Please. More. It burns. Do something." Her voice sounded high pitched and breathless as she panted and whimpered.

Travis's voice though, sounded harsh and gravelly. "Breathe, baby. Relax your bottom. I don't want to hurt you."

Stacy tried to relax her bottom muscles as much as possible. Travis's cock, so big and hot, pushed inside her so slowly she couldn't stand it. The head pass through the tight ring of muscle at her entrance. Her moans continued as he pushed forward more steadily now. He stroked inside her, forging deeper and deeper with each thrust.

"That's it, baby. Let me in. Oh, God, I need to be inside you this way. I won't hurt you, honey. I'll go nice and slow if it kills me."

He held her hips steady, his fingers biting into her as he used his thumbs to part her cheeks wider. Overloaded with sensation as he thrust all the way into her, she cried out. She clenched on him automatically, and she found she couldn't stop.

"Fuck." Travis growled. "You have the tightest ass in the world, baby." He leaned forward, covering her body with his once again. His breath at her ear felt hot, his words so erotic, fresh moisture dripped from her pussy.

"My cock is all the way inside that tight little virgin ass. Remember how slowly I pushed into you. If you ever talk about leaving the ranch again, I won't go so easy on you. You belong here.

I'm not letting you go, Stacy. Do you feel how deep I am inside you? So deep, so complete that it feels like I'm part of you? You're a part of me and you're staying that way."

He bit into her shoulder, his teeth sinking into her and holding her steady for his thrusts. His hand went around her and between her wide splayed thighs, pressing a rough finger against her clit.

He released her shoulder to growl in her ear. "Come. Let go for me."

The desperate need in his voice went straight to her head. Dazzled and overwhelmed, she shook with the force of the explosion inside her. She bucked and thrashed on Travis' thick steel, unable to stand the strength of it. Clenching repeatedly on the cock in her bottom, the muscles inside her burned even more. That sent her off again. She screamed her pleasure which just wouldn't stop.

Travis, swearing and groaning, held onto her sweat coated hips as he thrust hard and fast into her. His harsh, fierce growl came from deep within his chest, and she reveled in it.

He wrapped himself around her, covering her body completely with his own. They remained frozen that way for several minutes as their breathing gradually slowed and their bodies began to cool. She moaned when he slid from her.

He helped her to stand, pulling her in front of the window until he could see her face in the moonlight. Grabbing her hair, he pulled her head back, tilting her face to his. He crushed his lips to hers, pulling her tightly against him. Cupping her head with his big hand, he devoured her mouth, taking it over and over again.

A big shudder went through him and his mouth became gentler, his kisses lingering and slow until finally he lifted his head. Running his hands over her hair, he smiled.

Looking up at him, she bit back the words of love that almost sprang from her lips. She wanted more than anything to be able to stay here. Her time with each of them was precious to her. She would remember every second of it for the rest of her life.

But it only reinforced her decision to leave. She wouldn't be able to resist any of them.

When they all found out what she'd done, they would all think her a whore.

Why did she have to fall in love with *all* of them?

"What is it, baby?"

Startled out of her musings, Stacy shook her head. "Nothing. I just wish-"

Travis gripped her chin. "Don't *ever* threaten to leave again. You won't like what I'll do to you."

Chapter Four

Stacy woke the next morning, wincing at her sore bottom. Suddenly, the events of the previous night all came rushing back to her. Remembering the way Travis had taken over her made her smile. She'd wanted everything he'd had to give and had wanted to give everything in return.

Sitting up, she brushed the hair away from her face and sighed. She had felt the same way after Wolfe had taken her and the same after the night with Cash. And yet she'd betrayed each and every one of them.

Tears well up in her eyes. It just wasn't fair. Why did she have to love all three of them? Any one of them had always been more than enough man in her eyes. Why couldn't she have just fallen in love with one of them and have nothing more than brotherly affection for the others?

Had she become so starved for love because her father never gave her any?

Laying her head on her knees, she circled her arms around her legs and looked toward the window. She knew if she went over to it, she would see the yard full of ranch hands and at least one of her lovers.

One always stayed close to the house in case of emergencies and to take care of the million and one chores that had to be done. None of the ranch hands could ever slack off. The Dakota men watched every part of the ranch like hawks. Nothing escaped their notice.

How long would it be before one of them found out what she'd done?

She couldn't face them again. They'd always been able to read her. She would collapse under the weight of the guilt she now carried and they'd know the truth. She'd really done it this time. She wouldn't even be able to stay in Great Falls anymore. If any of them decided to come after her, she had to be gone. But where could she go?

* * * *

Wiping her forehead with the back of her hand, Stacy reached for a towel to start to dry some of the mounds of dishes she'd just washed. The work wasn't hard but it got hot in the kitchen. Right now she was grateful that she even had a job. She hadn't yet found a job as a secretary or receptionist and had been willing to work wherever she could.

Since she'd had to leave her other job with no notice, they wouldn't give her a letter of reference even after she'd explained the situation to them. She'd moved to a small town just south of Great Falls and had leased a small house. She'd lost the security deposit on her apartment, once again because of leaving with no notice. She wouldn't work as a dishwasher forever, but she had to do whatever became necessary to live.

She'd left the day after her night with Travis, knowing she couldn't sit at the dinner table with all of them ever again. She'd left a note for Rosa to find and took off like the hounds of hell were behind her.

Probably a good analogy.

It had been a little over a month since she'd gone, and she hoped that they had cooled down. She'd like to be able to call Rosa to talk to the older woman, but so far hadn't dared.

A week after she'd gone, her monthly flow had come right on time and she'd cried like a baby that she wouldn't have that part of Wolfe to keep with her. It would have been selfish, she knew, but she would have told him about it one day. Probably. With the marks already against her, what was one more?

"You look wilted, girl. You'd better get a good night's sleep tonight."

Stacy looked over at John, the friendly cook. "I will. I just have a few more resumes to send out."

"What? And leave all this?"

Stacy laughed as he'd meant her to and continued to dry and put away dishes.

John had been nice to her since she'd first started but the owner had been a bear. He yelled at the waitresses for not moving fast enough and took half of their tips. Nobody liked him and if it hadn't been for the good food and nice waitresses, the place would have already closed down. The customers couldn't stand him.

A lot like her father, Buck yelled unnecessarily. He liked the sound of his own voice, and he got on Stacy's nerves so much she had a headache every night when she left. She felt the same way with him as she had with her father. She couldn't wait to get away from him.

Shortly before closing time, she heard the bell on the door announce new customers. Great. They would have to stay late again tonight, and Buck didn't pay past the time the diner closed.

The diner suddenly got silent and John looked out the door to the front. "Whoever they are, I think Buck's in a lot of trouble if he opens his mouth."

"Where's Stacy?"

Stacy froze and almost dropped the plate she had been drying. Wolfe.

"Who are you and what do you want with her?" Buck's voice didn't carry its usual venom, and Stacy would have smiled if she hadn't been so scared.

Stacy glanced out the swinging door, hiding behind John and watched in amazement as Wolfe lifted Buck a good foot off the floor with one hand. Travis and Cash stood on each side of him, glaring at Buck.

"Where's Stacy?"

Buck, the rat, pointed to the back, and she saw all three lift their gazes directly to hers. Damn.

Wolfe dropped Buck to the floor as all three headed for her. Panicked, she took off, running out the back of the diner, hearing the sounds of their heavy boots closing in fast behind her. She cut across the parking lot in the back and kept going, her sneakers sliding on the damp grass.

A hand reached out as she passed a tree, grabbing her shirt and pulling her to a skidding halt. "Hey, pretty thing. What are you doing out here alone?" Smelling alcohol and sweat, she glanced at the man, who looked at her hungrily.

Looking over the man's shoulder, she saw Wolfe approach, Travis and Cash flanking him. Her mouth went dry when she saw the looks on their faces. They knew! She had no idea what they planned for her but it couldn't be good and she sure as hell didn't want to find out.

She didn't feel the least bit of fear for the man holding her and apparently he didn't like the fact that she all but ignored him. He looked over his shoulder, probably wondering what had her so scared and looked directly into the eyes of three very large Dakota men in a rage.

The man let go of her so fast she might have been on fire and took off, stumbling in his haste to get away. Cash flicked him a glance but none of the brothers moved to follow him. They all stood looking at her, and she trembled under their combined gazes. She started backing away again, watching them closely.

They all looked madder than hell and she knew that things would never be the same again. She'd ruined it all. Why hadn't they just stayed away? Why did they feel the need to punish her? Couldn't they just have called her a bitch and forgotten all about her?

No, not the Dakota men.

They made people pay for the smallest slight, and she had been naïve in thinking that they would let her get away with betraying them. She'd thought that with the history they had, they would have let her go but knew that she was really in big trouble.

She spun and took off again, blind fear ruling her feet, only taking about three steps before she found herself hauled up by a steel band at her waist. Travis. She fought uselessly, desperation giving her strength.

"Going somewhere, hellcat?" His low rumbled sounded close to her ear, holding onto her easily.

Finally she slumped, realizing the futility of fighting him. "I'm sorry," she whimpered.

"You're definitely gonna be sorry, little hellcat."

He tossed her over his shoulder, and they headed back the way they'd come, walking through the parking lot behind the diner and going up the alleyway between the buildings. Coming out at the front they moved to Wolfe's truck with Stacy bobbing sickeningly on Travis' shoulder. Shaking, she wondered what they would do to her.

Travis opened the back door and pushed her inside, climbing in behind her. Wolfe got behind the wheel and Cash sat in the passenger seat, turning to look at her accusingly before facing forward. The hurt in his eyes brought tears to her own.

Wolfe started the truck and turned, his big arm across the top of the front seat. "Are you pregnant?"

All three watched her intently, and she shook her head, lowering he eyes back to her lap. No one said a word as Wolfe pulled away from the curb. She kept her head down, not wanting to see the hurt and accusation on their faces and after only a few minutes, Wolfe pulled over and stopped the truck.

Stacy glanced up then, surprised that he had driven to the house she now rented. They knew where she lived. Why did that surprise her?

Travis half carried her, half dragged her out of the truck and followed Wolfe to the house, Cash following close behind them. When they got to the door, Wolfe held out his hand.

"My purse is back at the diner."

Stacy stood there, stunned to her toes, as he kicked the door with one big boot and sent it crashing in. He went in ahead of her with Travis nudging her forward to follow, holding her steady as she stumbled over the broken door. She turned to see Cash righting it before Travis nudged her again.

"Keep going, hellcat." The steel in his deep growl made her shudder and she fought to put one foot in front of the other. She deserved this and owed them the chance to yell at her. Knowing how badly she had to have hurt them, she would take whatever they dished out. Once they left, she wouldn't see them again.

Wolfe walked straight to her bedroom and sat on her bed, removing his boots and socks. He didn't even look at her as though knowing one of his brothers would catch her if she tried to bolt.

She stood there shaking as Travis also removed his boots and socks. Before he had finished, Wolfe's hand reached out with the speed of a rattler and grabbed her arm. He pulled her close and grabbing her shirt in his big hands, ripped it off of her. Her bra met the same fate.

He moved so fast she couldn't keep up with him as he tore at the fastenings of her jeans. He pulled them and her panties down to her knees in one strong jerk and tossed her over his lap. Oh God. One of them flipped on the light, and she knew they could all see her naked bottom, would all witness what would happen.

The other two had spanked her but it had been nothing like this. Wolfe never said a word, no warning, no erotic teasing. He just tossed her over his lap and started spanking her. Hard. One of the others grabbed her kicking feet and took the rest of her clothing off of her. It never slowed Wolfe down.

This spanking hurt. Her bottom was on fire, and he just kept going. She fought, she struggled, screaming at him the whole time. Finally spent, she lay docilely across his lap, whimpering. "I'm sorry. I'm so sorry." Whatever he did to her she more than deserved. He'd taken her virginity, and she'd betrayed him.

As soon as she'd stopped fighting, the spanking ended. His hand caressed the cheeks of her bottom and she winced at the heat. She deserved this from him after what she'd done. Now that he'd spanked her, they would all probably leave.

No one said a word for several long minutes as Wolfe caressed her heated bottom, spreading the heat to the place between her thighs. Impossible. After a spanking like that? It appeared that however any of them touched her, she couldn't help but respond.

"You left."

The unbelievable sadness in his voice had her throat clogging with tears. "I'm sorry."

"Why?"

Why? "You know why. It's why you're here. I betrayed you."

He lifted her to her feet with a speed that made her dizzy, standing her between his legs directly in front of him. She looked in his eyes and could see the love for her shining in them even now. But even he could never forgive her for this.

"Betrayed me?"

Stacy nodded, her face burning in shame. "I'm sorry. I couldn't help it. I love all three of you." A sob escaped as the extent of her actions had been spoken out loud.

Wolfe stared at her for so long that started to wonder if he would speak again or just walk out of the room. Finally he spoke. "Have you let anyone but Travis and Cash touch you?"

She frowned at him. "Of course not. Wasn't that enough?"

"Did you also think that you were betraying them?"

Stacy nodded.

"All three of us knew about the others the entire time."

Nothing he could have said would have surprised her more. "What? You mean I've been going around feeling like a piece of shit and all of you knew it the entire time?"

"Watch your mouth," Travis growled from his position across the room.

Stacy ignored him for now and kept her eyes on Wolfe. Right now he was the most dangerous one in the room.

"We know everything that goes on at the ranch and with you. All three of us have loved you for years. We've waited for you for years. We always knew that we would share you. You belong to all of us."

Stacy's knees buckled. "All three of you?"

Wolfe nodded, his eyes blazing.

Stacy put a hand over her mouth, looking at each one of them in turn. She could really have all three of them? A gulping sob broke rising from someplace deep inside her when she realized just what that meant. "I can live at the ranch with all three of you?"

Travis moved in behind her, running a hand over her warm bottom. "Yes, hellcat. You're going to marry Wolfe but you'll belong to all three of us."

Her eyes flicked to Cash to find him leaning against the bathroom doorway, smiling, obviously content to sit back and watch his brothers at work.

Her attention quickly went back to Wolfe when he stroked a nipple. "If it bothered you, and you thought you were betraying us, why didn't you come to us and tell us."

"I couldn't."

"So if you have a problem in the future, you're going to try to hide it from us?"

Stacy squirmed, not liking the direction this was going. "No. I just didn't know how to tell you. I hated keeping secrets from all of you."

Wolfe raised a brow at that and said nothing. Uh oh.

Travis leaned over her shoulder. "Do you really think you're going to get away with running from us, making us look for you a month before we could find you and keeping secrets from us?"

Stacy smiled hesitantly. "Just this time, right?"

Cash bared his teeth. "Wrong. Do you know how worried we were that you might be alone and pregnant? Do you have any idea of how often Rosa cried, afraid that we would never get you back? Do you know how many dirty looks we got from Dad because we hadn't told you everything from the beginning?"

Stacy latched onto that quickly. "See. It *is* partially your fault. If you had told me in the beginning that all three of you wanted me none of this would have happened."

Travis ran his hand threateningly over her bottom. "You had the chance to come to us and tell us what was bothering you and you didn't. What did I tell you would happen if you ran away again?"

Stacy shook her head, aware that standing here naked while they all remained dressed left her in a completely vulnerable position but relief made her giddy. "You said that I would be in trouble if I *threatened* to leave. I never threatened to, I just did it." She smiled at him but apparently he didn't appreciate her logic. Her smile fell.

Wolfe eyes glittered and the look on his face took her breath away. "Do you have any idea what we're going to do to you?"

Stacy shuddered, gulping and shook her head. With all three of them there she couldn't even imagine what they had in store for her. "Can I take a shower? I'm all sweaty."

Travis reached his hands around to cup her breasts, nuzzling her neck. "Later. You're going to get a helluva lot sweatier before we're through with you."

He pinched a nipple in each hand and she moaned, letting her head drop back against his chest. More moisture flowed from her slit. Wolfe's hand moved between her legs, she hoped he would think it came from her nipples being pinched and not his spanking. Her body blazed with heat, ultra sensitive, as she stood, for the first time, before all three of her lovers completely naked.

"You liked your spanking," he said softly, looking at her.

Damn. She kept silent and Travis pinched her nipples harder.

"Answer Wolfe, baby."

"He didn't ask me anything. Ohhh God. Yesss! I liked my spanking. But it hurt."

Wolfe's lips twitched. "It was supposed to. You're lucky I went easy on you. I won't go so easy if you ever try to run away again. *Talk* to us, Stacy. We've always been there for you. That certainly isn't going to change."

Stacy's eyes widened. *That was easy?*

With his hands on her bottom, the heat of them making it burn even more, Wolfe lifted her dripping pussy to his mouth. Travis lifted her and she dropped her head back onto his shoulder. Wolfe didn't tease like Cash, but went straight for what he wanted, immediately pushing his tongue inside her. He thrust into her several times before moving to her clit. The jolts of pleasure from her nipples being pinched made her clit throb even more. When Wolfe closed his mouth over it, she gasped. He held it with his teeth, causing her whole body to shake as he sucked it hard into his mouth. She came hard and fast, digging her nails into Travis' biceps as she held on tightly.

Wolfe lifted his mouth from her and moved aside, motioning for Travis to lay her on the bed. Three sets of hands ran over her, three pairs of lips touched her, and she writhed on the bed as her system went on overload.

One kiss slid into another, a hand at one breast and a hot mouth on the other had her body struggling to catch up. A thick finger pressed into her pussy, and she lifted herself, trying to move on it. When it withdrew she whimpered until it was replaced by a thick cock.

"Oh. Fuck. She's so tight." Cash.

Wolfe and Travis leaned on an elbow on either side of her, their gazes moving from her face to where their brother thrust into her.

She loved the feeling of all three of them being a part of their lovemaking. Wolfe watched her, his eyes indulgent as the pleasure took her higher and higher. Travis looked down at her, his eyes fierce, his hands sliding back and forth between her breasts and pinching her nipples. Cash's face looked set in stone as he thrust into her hard, his pace quickening. She held onto both Wolfe and Travis's shoulders as Cash's thrusts threatened to push her across the bed.

When Wolfe's hand moved across her stomach and lower, she whimpered, knowing what came next. Her eyes became fixed on his as he touched a finger to her clit and pressed. Cash's movements provided the friction and her climax bloomed from her clit outward, sizzling along her skin. She grabbed onto both Travis and Wolfe even harder, groaning into Wolfe's mouth when he covered it with his own.

She heard Cash's harsh groan. He tightened his hands on her hips, and with one last thrust, he emptied himself inside her. Cash held her against him, running his hand over her stomach. Wolfe lifted his head and slid his own hand from where it had covered her clit, to smooth over her stomach. Several minutes passed as they stroked and fondled her.

"What if I get pregnant?"

She thrilled at the look of raw heat that flared in Wolfe's eyes and turned to see that both Travis and Cash had a similar look in their own.

Wolfe gripped her chin and turned her to face him. "We would love it."

"But how would we know which one of you is the father?"

"We will all be the fathers of all of your babies." He smiled so sweetly at her and traced her bottom lip.

"Can this really work?"

With a finger on her cheek, Travis turned her to face him. "We'll make it work."

She kissed each of them and complained that now she desperately needed a shower. Laughing, she went into the shower and wasn't surprised when someone walked into the bathroom to join her.

Travis pushed aside the curtain and got in, and her knees went weak as she saw him completely naked for the first time. She had taken *that* in her bottom? Travis obviously read her face because he chuckled. "Don't worry, you already know you can take me. Come here so I can wash you."

He soaped her everywhere, and she'd become a quivering mass of jelly by the time he'd finished. She grabbed the soap and used the excuse of washing him to be able to touch him all over. She couldn't get over his chest and back. Like his brothers, years of working the ranch had left their bodies roped with muscle. She'd seen many cowboys take off their shirts in the heat of the day, and none could compare to her men.

Her men. She loved the sound of that. She reached down to take Travis's cock in her hand. It looked hot and hard and thick, and she wanted it. Now.

Travis grabbed her hand and pulled it away from his impressive erection. "No, you don't. You'll just have to wait. Get out of here and let me shower."

She opened the curtain, surprised that Wolfe stood waiting for her. He had undressed except for his boxers, which tented nicely. He held out a towel for her and dried her. Picking her up, he carried her back into the bedroom. She looked down at the bed in surprise to see a towel laid out on it along with a can of shaving cream and a razor.

"What are you going to do?" She hated the sound of the little girl fear in her voice but couldn't help it.

Wolfe laid her gently on the towel, opening the one he'd already put around her. "I'm going to shave your pussy. I want you to keep it bare for us. You'll love it. It'll make your soft little pussy even softer and much more sensitive."

Wolfe had spoken more tonight than she had heard him speak in a long time and almost every time he opened his mouth something dark or erotic came out of it. Cash had gone into the bathroom and came back with a damp towel as Wolfe spread shaving cream on her. "Lay very still, little one. I don't want to cut you."

Her body began to tremble but she stayed as still as she could as Wolfe slid the razor over her again and again, ridding her of her curls. Travis had come out of the bathroom by then and watched raptly as Wolfe revealed her now bare pussy. Cash went into the bathroom and she dimly heard the shower start again.

"Beautiful," Travis murmured after Wolfe had wiped away the last of the cream.

Wolfe threw the wet towels toward the bathroom and Travis lowered his head to her slit. His mouth felt even more devastating on her highly sensitive flesh. Travis didn't tease her with his tongue the way Cash had. No, not Travis. He ate at her hungrily as though starved, the way Wolfe had. He ravaged her, sending her higher and higher with every devastating lick, every scrape of his teeth.

He threw her over so quickly that she hadn't even known she'd been close, then kept going, stabbing his tongue inside her over and over until she thrashed wildly beneath him. Her juices flowed as fast as he could consume them. When her body gathered again, he lifted his head.

She twisted frantically. "I want more."

He chuckled and grabbed her by the waist, lifting her high as he lay back on the bed and poised her pussy over the head of his cock. She gasped at both the quickness of his move and the feel of his cock pressing into her. He lowered her inch by inch on his length until he became fully imbedded inside her.

She grabbed onto his shoulders and started to move but he held her still, his face tight with tension. "Don't move, little hellcat."

"But I want to—"

She froze as Wolfe moved in behind her.

"Look what I found." She turned to see him holding up a bottle of baby oil from her bathroom.

"Oh God."

Wolfe pushed her hair to one side and leaned down to kiss her neck. "Trust us." With a hand to her back Wolfe lowered her to Travis' chest.

Travis wrapped his arms around her and held her tightly. His hot cock shifted inside her.

The first touch of Wolfe's oil coated finger on her bottom hole had her gripping Travis tighter and burying her face against his chest. "I'm scared."

"We've got you, baby. Relax those muscles. Remember?"

Her grip on Travis got tighter when Wolfe pressed the oil into her puckered opening. When he began stroking inside her, she moaned and her pussy clenched on Travis. She heard his low curses and groans as though from a distance as Wolfe began to press his cock into her opening.

She jolted as the head pushed against the tight ring of muscle, but Travis' arms around her held her steady.

"Damn. If that isn't a beautiful sight." Cash moved beside them, sitting on the bed next to them. He stroked her back. "Easy, kitten. Loosen up so Wolfe can get inside your tight little bottom."

She heard the strain in his voice and knew that watching Wolfe pushing his cock into her bottom had to be arousing him. Wolfe steadily pressed into her, and she whimpered. "It burns. It's too much."

Travis lifted her face to his and nipped her lips, forcing them open and taking possession of her mouth. Cash's hand covered her breast, tugging at a nipple, making her body clench. Both Travis and Wolfe groaned as she tightened on them but she couldn't seem to stop. She whimpered into Travis's mouth as the burn got hotter.

Wolfe began to stroke in and out of her, and she lifted slightly.

Holding onto Travis's shoulders she began to move with his thrusts.

Travis took over, gripping her hips, and he and Wolfe set up a rhythm. Every stroke took Wolfe a little deeper inside her, until finally he'd become seated to the hilt, Wolfe's hands on her shoulders pushing her down onto him.

With both of their cocks all the way inside her, Stacy began to shake. Her whimpers and moans echoed in the room along with the groans of her lovers. She felt full to bursting, fuller than she'd ever thought she could be. The erotic pleasure-pain and having all three of them touching her cut through all her inhibitions and made her wild.

Stacy could do nothing but go for the ride. Cash had one hand on her back, stroking her while the other teased and tormented her already too sensitive nipples.

With her pussy bare, the friction on her clit increased and within only a few more strokes, her body gathered and tightened, then exploded. She screamed out her pleasure, almost overwhelmed by it. It went on and on and wouldn't stop. She clenched on both hard cocks thrusting into her, and it intensified the pleasurable-pain. Another climax hit her before the first could diminish.

Her screams spurred her lovers on and their thrusts became almost violent. When she tightened on them again, their roars of pleasure filled the room as they held themselves deeply inside her. Their cocks pulsed as they shot their hot seed into her.

She collapsed onto Travis's chest. Wolfe's lips moved on her back as he withdrew from her. She shuddered when the head of his cock passed the tight opening, and Travis's arms came around her.

He nuzzled her forehead as he stroked her back and she snuggled closer. With his arms wrapped around her and the heat of his body along hers, she was warm and sated. She never wanted to move again.

Almost asleep, she grumbled when Travis lifted her. "Come on, little hellcat. It's time to go home."

"Tomorrow," she mumbled, almost asleep.

He stood her up, chuckling and steadying her when she swayed. "We have a ranch to run. Come on, baby. Cash will help you get dressed while Wolfe and I carry your stuff to the car. You can sleep in my arms on the way home."

Stacy opened her eyes. "Home. I like the sound of that."

Wolfe came out of the bathroom. "That's why we bought the ranch from your dad. We knew you loved it and wanted it to be a home for you."

Stacy looked at each of them. "I love all of you so much." She went to each of them, kissing each of them softly. Suddenly bursting with energy, she scrambled to get dressed. "Come on. Hurry up. I want to go home."

* * * *

Stacy woke the next day with bright sunshine coming through her bedroom window. They'd gotten in late the night before. She'd fallen asleep in the car and when they got home, Wolfe had carried her straight up to her bedroom. He'd tried to help her undress but Rosa had shooed him away and stayed to help Stacy herself.

She took her shower and got dressed and started down the stairs, pressing a hand to her nervous stomach. The only thing now that could interfere with her happiness would be if Rosa or Rex had a problem with her relationship with all three men.

Walking into the kitchen, Stacy approached Rosa hesitantly. "Rosa?"

Rosa beamed and turned to her enveloping her in a big hug. Rosa's hugs always smelled like cinnamon, and Stacy closed her eyes at the wonderful familiarity. "It's about time you came back. Those boys haven't been fit company since you took off." She wagged her finger at Stacy.

"No, ma'am. I'm sorry I left the way I did. But you know why I had to leave, don't you?"

"Sure, 'cause those boys didn't tell you the truth about all three of them lovin' you. I heard them fight with Rex about it. Well, not exactly fight. You know Rex. He said what he had to and gave them dirty looks until they found you."

Stacy took a deep breath. "Do you think I'm bad because I love all three of them?"

"Bad? Baby, with the mean old father you had, you deserve every bit of love you can get. Those boys love you to death. Always have. And you love them. Do they make you happy?"

Stacy giggled. "When they're not making me crazy."

Rosa nodded. "That's just the way it should be. They hired some guys to come in and fix up the master bedroom. Took all of your daddy's stuff and threw it away. They said they wanted to start over."

Stacy's eyes burned, touched that they had thought of that. "So you're happy for me?"

Rosa clucked. "Of course, you silly girl. Now go out there and say hi to Rex. He's missed you."

Stacy bussed Rosa's cheek and skipped outside to see Rex standing at the fence, his arms draped over the top. She stepped onto the bottom rung so she would be high enough to kiss his cheek. He kept his eyes forward as she touched her lips to his leathery skin. She saw his lips twitch but he didn't say a word. Dropping back down, she stood beside him.

Looking out into the yard she saw all three of her men on their horses. They all started toward her when they saw her.

"Been waitin' for you to get up," Rex murmured.

"Who, you?"

"Nope, my sons. None of them wanted to leave the yard 'til they saw you this morning. Rosa's keepin' them out of your bedroom 'til the wedding. Better be soon or we'll never get any work done around here."

She saw her men advancing and couldn't keep from grinning at them or at their father. "That's the most I've heard you talk in a long time." She giggled. "Does that mean you don't have a problem with me taking all three of your sons off the market in one fell swoop?" She carefully kept her tone teasing but her gut tightened anxiously, waiting for his response, watching out of the corner of her eye as Wolfe, Travis and Cash approached.

Rex looked over at her, and she was surprised to see the sheen in his eyes. "My sons have always loved you, and you've always loved them. I hated that bully who sired you. I've considered you my daughter for years. Might as well make it legal."

With a sob, she threw herself at him, and found herself enveloped in a hard hug. Looking up she saw her men staring at her, love and possessiveness glittering in their eyes.

Rex nudged her. "Go on. If you don't kiss those boys good morning, we'll never get any work done around here."

Stacy laughed as she climbed over the fence and flew to her Dakota men.

THE END

Siren Publishing

Ménage Amour

Dakota
Ranch
Crude

DAKOTA HEAT ANTHOLOGY 2

Leah Brooke

DAKOTA RANCH CRUDE

Dakota Heat Anthology 2

LEAH BROOKE
Copyright © 2009

Chapter One

Samantha Cross fumbled with her keys as she rushed to unlock the door. The phone rang two more times before she managed to get inside. She rushed to it, hoping it was Petey.

"Hello?"

"Sam, it's me."

"Petey. Thank God! I've been trying to call you. Two men showed up at the diner looking for you. Where—"

"Sam, shut up and listen. I'm in jail."

"What? What happened? For what? Oh God! Petey, what did you do?"

"Right away you believe the worst! I'm already guilty, right? I'm in jail because I'm trying to protect your ass and right away it's my fault."

Samantha closed her eyes, mentally counting to ten. Nothing had ever been Petey's fault. She sighed. "Okay, Petey. Why are you in jail?"

"I got caught trying to steal a bull."

"What?"

"Listen, I only did it because of you! You know those two men that came looking for me? I met them in a bar and borrowed money from them. I had a sure bet at the racetrack and the fucking horse stumbled."

Samantha moved to close the door and plopped into a nearby chair, suddenly feeling very old. "So you lost it?"

"It's not my fault! You're the one that keeps pestering me for money for the fucking bills. I only gambled to get you your fucking money so I don't have to hear about it anymore."

Samantha leaned forward, rubbing her forehead where a dull throb had settled over her right eye. "So you tried to steal from your employers to pay them back?"

"Yeah. If I don't pay them back, they're gonna come after you. That's probably why they came to the diner. They want to make sure they know who you are. They asked if you're my sister, right?"

Samantha stood and began to pace, a feeling of dread settling low in her stomach. "Yes, they did. But why would they come after me if you're the one that borrowed the money?"

"To make sure I pay them! Jesus, you're stupid sometimes. If I don't get them their money, they said they would break both your legs."

Samantha gasped, horrified. She ran to the door to make sure she'd locked it. "Petey, what have you done?"

"Just come get me out of this fucking jail! Come bail me out and I'll take care of it."

When he told her how much bail money she'd need, Samantha groaned. "Petey, I don't have that kind of money. I—"

"I've been sending you money every fucking week. You'd better come up with it."

"Petey, this is your mess—" She heard a car door slam and pulled the phone away from her ear as Petey shouted and cursed at her. Running to the window, her eyes went wide as the two men from the diner approached her apartment building. Panic set it. "Petey! Those two men are here."

She dropped the phone, grabbed her keys and purse and raced out. She ran across the hall and banged on her friend's door. "Donna! It's Samantha. Let me in."

When the door opened, Samantha ran through it, closing it behind her. She shook so hard she couldn't turn the lock.

"Sam, what's going on?"

Finally getting the door locked, she gripped her friend's hand. Donna's face blurred as tears filled her eyes. "Shh! I'll explain. Just be really quiet."

Samantha moved to the peephole and looked out just in time to see the men approach her door. She'd never been so scared. What the hell had Petey gotten them into this time?

Despite wearing suits, both men looked cold and ruthless. A glimpse of their eyes sent a chill through her. A whimper escaped and she slapped a hand over her mouth, afraid they would hear her.

"Samantha," Donna whispered.

Samantha spun and slapped her free hand over her friend's mouth, shaking her head as tears ran down her face.

Donna's eyes widened and she nodded.

Samantha heard a crash and released her friend to spin back to the door and look out the peephole again. Her apartment door stood open and she watched the men go inside. Another whimper escaped when she realized just how close they'd come to getting to her.

Donna pushed her out of the way to look out. She turned back to Samantha, her eyes huge. "We have to call the police."

Another noise from the hallway had Samantha flying back to look out. The two men came back out of her apartment, leaving the door wide open, and started back down the stairs.

As soon as they moved out of sight, Samantha rushed to the window, careful to stand to the side where they couldn't see her. Not until they'd gotten into their car and driven away did she realize she'd been holding her breath.

"Sam, what's going on?"

Samantha ran to the door. "Let me know if they come back."

Instead of staying behind, Donna followed her as she ran back across the hall and into her apartment.

"Sam, damn it. What's going on?"

Samantha explained as Donna followed her around her apartment as she looked for anything out of place. Since Donna already knew about Petey, the explanation didn't take long.

"Damn it, Sam. You have enough to worry about without Petey getting into trouble again.

They both came to an abrupt halt when they reached Samantha's bedroom. The men had used her lipstick to write on her mirror.

"WE'LL BE BACK"

Samantha's legs gave way and she sank onto the edge of her bed. "Oh God."

She wrapped her arms around herself as chills wracked her body. "I've got to get out of here."

Shooting to her feet, she hurried to her closet, took out her suitcases, and began to throw clothes into them haphazardly.

Donna rushed to help. "Where are you going to go?"

Samantha snapped one lid closed as Donna threw the contents of her underwear drawer into the other case. "I've got to get Petey out of jail. Then I'll figure out the rest."

"How are you going to do that? You don't have enough money. I'd give it to you if I had it, but I don't."

Samantha grabbed one of the suitcases and her purse while Donna followed her with the other. "I'm going to have to go see Petey's employers, the men who had him arrested, and see if they'll drop the charges."

* * * *

Samantha eased off the accelerator, leaning forward to look up at the large sign to her right. "Dakota Ranch." Turning her little compact down the long drive, she admired the lush green lawn and mature trees. With the exception of the asphalt drive, this could be a scene from a hundred years ago.

Driving closer, she couldn't help but fall in love with the huge stucco house situated at the end of the driveway. The big porch that ran along the entire front managed to make the house look homey despite its size. It and all of the outbuildings had been painted a stark white.

A large stable that had what looked like dozens of cowboys all around it stood to the right. Several of the cowboys rode horses inside the post and rail fence. She assumed they were being 'exercised' as her brother called it. What kind of exercise did a horse need, for God's sake? It's a horse.

She didn't see any of the cattle that her brother had told her the ranch had become well known for, so she assumed the cows, bulls, steers or whatever had to be off playing somewhere else.

Samantha knew dairy products and cuts of beef. That was the beginning and the end of her knowledge of cows.

Everything looked to be well cared for, and the whole place just screamed money. Great. She'd imagined having to deal with some tobacco spitting cowboys. Instead she'd be dealing with some pot bellied know-it-all with a cigar sticking out of his mouth.

She knew nothing of ranches, nothing of animals or the great outdoors and had no desire to ever learn.

Her brother, however, knew more about horses and cattle and loved to work with them. She loved her little brother dearly, but Petey had always been like their father, continually getting into some kind of trouble. Samantha felt like she'd spent her whole life cleaning up their messes. Well, at least she didn't have to worry about getting daddy out of trouble anymore.

Pulling up to the front of the circular drive, Samantha pressed a hand to her stomach and took a deep breath. She had to make the Montgomery brothers understand. She had no choice. Petey had gotten them both into big trouble this time. When she opened the door and got out of the car, the heat nearly overwhelmed her. Riding in the air conditioned car, she'd forgotten how hot it was outside.

Straightening her sundress, she grabbed her purse and climbed the steps to the porch, her high heels clicking on the wood.

Her eyes widened as she took in the size of the house up close. Jeez, she'd hate like hell to be the one that had to clean this place.

Trying to get up the courage to knock, she looked around and absolutely fell in love with the porch. The wooden swing looked like the perfect place to sit and just watch the world go by. It would seat at least three people and she could just imagine lying on it as the swing moved with the breeze and settling down for a nap. An assortment of all weather furniture sat in clusters nearby. She could spend hours out here. The shade made it several degrees cooler and she could feel a light breeze blowing. She closed her eyes and enjoyed the touch of it over her heated skin.

"What do you want?"

Samantha spun at the deep growl and barely suppressed as gasp when she saw the most unbelievably gorgeous man she'd ever laid eyes on. About six feet of hard packed muscle stood just inside the screen door, eyeing her coolly and sipping coffee from a thick mug.

Brown, sun streaked hair fell rakishly over his forehead and just skimmed his shoulders. An unbuttoned chambray shirt hung open and she couldn't help but stare. Her eyes zeroed in on his chest, tanned and clearly delineated with muscle, sprinkled with dark, silky looking hair that she just itched to touch. A pair of well worn jeans hung from lean hips.

"I asked you what you wanted."

Samantha gulped as she looked up into eyes the color of milk chocolate. This man could be on the cover of any of the erotic novels she loved to read. Her mouth watered just looking at him. When he smiled at her mockingly, dimples slashed his cheeks and even white teeth appeared between lips so firm and soft looking, she found herself wondering what they would feel like on hers. Good Lord. It should be against the law for a man to be this beautiful.

His face hardened at her continued silence and he raised a brow.

Samantha had to clear her throat before speaking. Wiping her suddenly damp palms down her sundress, she finally found her voice. "Hello. I'm Samantha Cross. I'm looking for Mr. Montgomery, either one of them."

"I'm Jackson Montgomery. What. Do. You. Want?"

This man is one of the Montgomery brothers?

Get the drool off your chin, Sam, and plead your case!

Thoughts of the men who'd come to her apartment and the message they'd left raced through her mind and she sobered. She cleared her throat again, hating that she had to talk to him through a screen door. "I'm here about my brother."

His face tightened even more. "You're Pete Cross's sister?"

Fighting the urge to shift her feet, she nodded. "I'd like to talk to you about him."

He continued to stare at her as he sipped his coffee. He looked her over, his gaze caressing her body from top to bottom and back again. Her body heated and tingled and she struggled not to fidget. Her breasts felt swollen and she knew her nipples poked at the front of her dress. Damn.

"What are you offering?"

She couldn't have heard him right. "Excuse me?"

"You heard me. I appreciate a good lay as much as the next guy. I gotta tell you though, my brother and I share."

Where the surge of lust came from she had no idea, but she managed to tamp it down and firm her voice. "Mr. Montgomery, I'm here to talk to you or your brother about Petey. Since you apparently consider this a joke, perhaps it might be better if I talk to your brother. I hope *he* takes things a little more seriously."

For the first time, she saw actual humor on his face. "Oh, Shayne is a *lot* more serious than I am."

He pushed open the screen door and stood aside so she could enter. He hadn't moved quite enough for her to pass without touching him and she sucked in a breath as her nipples brushed against his chest. The electric jolt shot straight to her slit and she quickly stepped away from him. Those incredible dimples slashed again as he gestured with the hand holding the coffee mug. "Right this way. I've got to see this."

Samantha walked in the direction he'd indicated, moving into a room that appeared to be their office. She came to an abrupt halt when she saw another man seated behind the desk, cursing into the phone. He slammed the receiver into its base as they approached.

"Another one of your girlfriends?"

Samantha bristled at his tone, even as the dark timber of it drew her. *Get a grip, Sam.* This man could never be called handsome, not by any stretch of the word. His hard features had been carved too roughly for that. No expression, no warmth, no surprise. Just *hard.*

His eyes were so dark they looked nearly black and ice cold. They crinkled at the corners, probably from squinting, certainly not from smiling, and he had the most incredible eyelashes she'd ever seen. His eyes stayed hooded, as though the lush thickness of those lashes weighed them down, but the sharpness of his gaze told her he never missed a thing.

What really grabbed her attention and kept her frozen in place was the sheer size of him. Even sitting behind a desk, he looked massive with shoulders wider than any she had ever seen before. When he picked up his own mug, it looked like a child's teacup. Without a doubt, he was the most formidable looking man she'd ever met. And she needed his help. Great.

"No," she heard Jackson say from behind her. "This is Samantha Cross, Pete's sister. Samantha, this is my brother, Shayne Montgomery."

Samantha gripped her purse tighter and fought the urge to fidget under the larger man's stare. His eyes hardened even more as he dropped his pen on his desk and leaned back. The chair groaned at the movement. "What do you want?"

The deep rumble in his tone made her shudder, amazing her that not only fear had caused it. He had to be hands down the most masculine man she'd ever met and her body reacted to him too strongly for her own piece of mind. The stress must be getting to her. She understood her attraction to Jackson. Of course she would be attracted to a man who looked like a damned Greek God. But to be attracted to this man, too? Must be the stress.

Jeez, Sam. Plead your case and get the hell out of here!

* * * *

Shayne Montgomery looked up at the woman Jackson had escorted into his study. He had paperwork to finish before he could get back outside and didn't have time for interruptions. The phone call had pissed him off. Why couldn't that asshole take no for an answer? When he'd heard his brother say that a woman had just pulled in, he'd figured it had to be another one of Jackson's girlfriends. Christ, sometimes they showed up two and three at a time.

Hearing her scathing retort to his brother's demand to know what she would offer had intrigued him. Women never said no to Jackson. He'd looked up as she'd walked in and had become hard as a rock the instant those violet eyes had met his.

Samantha Cross had the face of an angel and the body of a siren. Her features looked delicate, almost fragile, except for that mouth. Her wide violet eyes, button nose and sexy as hell flush on her creamy skin brought every ounce of protective instinct inside him to the surface. Christ, what he wouldn't give to be able to have a woman that looked like this one.

Her pale blonde hair looked like a curtain of silk and he wanted to bury his face in it. Or see it fanned out on his pillow. Or fist it in his hands as he shoved his cock into that gorgeous mouth and fucked it. He couldn't keep his eyes off that mouth. He could nibble at those soft, full lips all day and never get tired of it. He hated the lipstick that coated them. If she belonged to him, her lips would be that lush pink permanently from his kisses and would be swollen even more.

She had the mouth of a seductress.

A mouth worth killing for.

Her nipples poked at her dress, and he knew that just being around Jackson had caused it. He wondered what color those beaded little nipples would be. What sounds would she make as he tugged them with his lips?

Watching Jackson lead her to the sofa, he couldn't keep his eyes from the sway of her hips as she walked across the room. The full, rounded globes of her ass made him want to bend her over the back of the sofa and spread them.

Do not go there!

He hated skinny women and this one had lots of curves. His cock jumped, thinking about having that ass bare and ready for him to explore. He'd bet his prized bull that those globes would be firm but soft, pale against his hand. He would spend time learning that ass with his hands and lips, working his way to her puckered opening.

Snap out of it, Shayne.

Jackson looked over his shoulder to frown at him disapprovingly, probably because of his brusque manner. Hell, Jackson had always been more polite than he could ever be. Jackson did all the smiling.

His brother had definitely gotten all the charm in the family. And all the looks.

Shayne had accepted long ago that women like her only wanted men like Jackson. He had no illusions about his looks and his size, and his need to dominate in the bedroom drove most women away. Women only wanted him for two things, his cock and his money.

He had to find out whatever the fuck this woman wanted from them and get her the hell out of here. Having her here brought needs to the surface, needs he tried his best to ignore. They reminded him why he could never have a woman like her.

"Your brother's a cattle thief."

Samantha looked over at the giant sitting behind the desk. "He's not really a cattle thief. Not at all."

* * * *

When he just lifted a brow at her, she scooted forward in her seat. She had to make them listen. "He's not, I swear." She took a deep breath. "Please, let me explain." When they both just continued to stare at her, she began.

"My mother died early this year after a long illness." Her voice shook whenever she talked about her mother and she determinedly firmed it. "My father took off and Petey and I took care of her until she died. The medical bills kept piling up, so we sold everything, including the house to pay off as much as we could." She paused to look at each of them.

Jackson nodded for her to continue, but neither showed the slightest flicker of emotion. Great. She just had to get through to them or she didn't know what she would do. "Petey had been working as a dishwasher and when he saw your ad, he came here to work because it paid more. He's always loved being around horses. Our neighbors had them."

Their continued silence and stares flustered her. The way Shayne Montgomery stared at her had her barely resisting the urge to bolt. His dark eyes had darkened even more. His unwavering stare made her edgy, reminding her of a wild animal. She trembled, afraid he would pounce at any sudden movement. Unable to sit any longer, she stood and moved slowly to the window, keeping him in her peripheral vision the entire time.

Something about him just pulled at her. She couldn't help but wonder what it would feel like to be held by this man. His raw masculinity nearly overwhelmed her.

Meanwhile, Jackson kept staring at her as he might a bug under a microscope. She carefully avoided his sharp gaze, which made her feel as though he mentally stripped her bare.

How the hell could she be so consumed by sexual tension while fighting for her brother's life? How the hell could she stand here wanting to actually know what it felt like to be in Shayne's huge arms, to give in to the erotic pull of Jackson's stare while she had this threat over her head and was scared to death?

Stop it, Sam!

She took a deep breath and cleared her throat. It took her a minute to gather her thoughts. "I stayed and kept my job. Petey's been sending me what money he could and we've been trying to pay off the medical bills." She rubbed her stomach where it churned every time she thought about what Petey had done. "Petey started gambling to raise the money. He thought he could raise the money faster that way. Instead, he lost."

She rubbed her stomach again. It had almost become a habit. "He got involved with some bad people, borrowed money from them to gamble some more and lost *it*. The men he borrowed from threatened to hurt me if he didn't pay them back. He panicked. That's why he tried to steal your cow. To sell it to pay them off."

"Bull," Shayne murmured.

"It's true!" Samantha moved to the desk, leaning over it toward Shayne. His eyes flared and she hurriedly straightened. She took a deep breath and looked at them both pleadingly. She *had* to make them believe her. "He only did it to protect me!"

Jackson's lips twitched. "Shayne didn't mean he didn't believe you. Your brother tried to steal a bull, not a cow."

"Oh." When neither man spoke, she could feel her nerves stretch almost to the breaking point. Jackson's eyes kept sliding from her to Shayne and back again, but Shayne's gaze stayed steady on her. Just when she thought she couldn't stand another second of the deafening silence, Shayne spoke.

"I understand why Pete did what he did."

Samantha sighed, relief making her lightheaded. She moved to the sofa and dropped back in her seat. "Thank you."

"But," he continued. "I don't know exactly what you expect us to do about it."

Samantha looked from one to the other, frowning. "I want you to drop the charges against him."

"And then what?" Shayne asked softly. Too softly. She felt goosebumps break out on her arms. She crossed her arms over her chest and rubbed them, covering her beaded nipples from their gazes. What would that voice sound like in the bedroom, in the dark, against her—?

Breathe Sam! She took another deep breath. "I don't understand." Hell, she'd forgotten what they'd been talking about.

Shayne sighed. "Your brother seems to have a penchant for trouble. If we drop the charges against him, he'll get out of jail, but then what? He's already put you in danger and is deeper in debt than before. What do you think would happen if he got loose?"

Samantha blinked. His continued stare flustered her more than she wanted to admit. "But while he's in jail, he can't make any money. I've got to get those people paid off as soon as possible! I can't keep looking over my shoulder while I'm working to pay these people back *and* come up with the money for the medical bills."

Shayne inclined his head. "True." The silence stretched again. "How much money are we talking about?"

Samantha sighed and looked back down at her lap "After selling the house and everything, we still owe a little over a hundred thousand dollars in medical bills."

"And the other?"

Samantha rubbed her stomach and looked up. "Petey originally borrowed twenty five thousand but he said with interest it's now close to fifty thousand dollars."

Jackson whistled at the amount before his face tightened in anger. He looked over at his brother. "Pete tried to steal a bull worth over a million dollars to pay a debt of a hundred and fifty grand?"

Samantha's mouth dropped open. "A million dollars? For a cow?"

"Bull," Shayne corrected absently.

Samantha watched them both apprehensively as some sort of male communication passed between them that she had no hope of understanding. Looking at her lap and noticing that her knuckles had turned white where she gripped her purse, she made a conscious effort to loosen them. Her nerves couldn't take much more. Would they let Petey go? She didn't know what she'd do if they refused her. But even if they did let him go, how would they come up with the money they owed? Shayne had been right about that. No matter how she looked at it, she couldn't see a way out. One problem at a time. First, she had to get her brother out of jail.

She looked up to find them both watching her. Her face burned, and she wondered what they were thinking. Forcing herself to sit still, she waited.

"Can you cook?"

Samantha blinked at Jackson's unexpected question. Without meaning to, her eyes flew to Shayne, taken aback when his face hardened even more.

Looking away hurriedly, she forced her gaze back to Jackson, trying hard to ignore the heated amusement in his eyes. "Yes. I've always loved to cook. That's what I do. I cook in a diner. Why?"

"I have a solution to your problem."

Shayne's warning growl shocked her and made her tremble. If either saw it, she hoped they would think fear caused it. That growl did something strange to her insides. She tightened her thighs against the rush of heat that soaked her panties.

She met Jackson's gaze, struggling to keep her tone neutral. "You do? What is it?"

"My brother and I will drop the charges against your brother and pay off your debts."

Samantha narrowed her eyes. "Just like that? What do you want in return?"

Jackson's dimples appeared again. "I see you're not as gullible as your brother. That's good. Your brother will work here, properly supervised of course, for room and board during the next year."

Samantha slumped in relief. They'd believed her. Petey could keep his job. She would also send money and they would no longer have men threatening her. "Oh, thank—"

"And *you*," Jackson continued as though she hadn't spoken, "will quit your job at the diner to live and work here."

"What?" Samantha stared at him, stunned.

"You heard me. Our housekeeper retired. You can take her place. You'll get room and board like your brother."

She looked over at Shayne's unreadable expression before looking back at Jackson, who'd leaned back against the arm of the sofa. "For how long?"

"One year."

"A year!" Samantha jumped up and moved back to the window. How the hell could she live here with these two for a whole year without going out of her mind? Her panties had been soaked since she'd walked through the door. They both affected her too much to ignore. This stuff didn't happen to her. But how else could she get out of this mess?

Samantha closed her eyes. "Shouldn't I speak to your wives about working here?" *Please let them be married.* Then she knew she could resist them.

"We're not married," Jackson grinned and she felt it all the way to her core. "I already told you, we like to share. One woman would have to put up with both of us."

"That's enough, Jackson," Shayne growled and stood. "Don't threaten her with me. She's all yours."

Samantha looked back out the window, trying to hide her surprise and surge of lust. *They shared?* It was a fantasy straight out of her books. Oh God, what would it feel like to have them both make love to her, one in her pussy and the other…Oh Lord, she couldn't even imagine.

"A year isn't so bad to work off a debt like that. Besides, what are your options?"

Startled when Jackson's voice jerked her out of her musings, she took a shuddering breath before answering. She needed a few minutes alone. Why she reacted this way she had no idea but she just had to get over it. "Just to be your housekeeper, nothing else?"

"Your job is just to take care of the house and the meals." His eyes twinkled in amusement. "Anything else is your own choice and not part of the debt."

Damn. She really had no other option, but the way Jackson kept looking at her unsettled the hell out of her. She tried to ignore the burning looks and the way he appeared to undress her with his eyes. Samantha looked over to see Shayne moving around his desk. Her eyes widened when she really got a look at his size. She'd never seen a man that big! Easily over six and a half feet tall, he looked to be pure solid muscle. His chest looked like a barrel and his thighs like tree trunks.

Closer now, she got a better look at those hooded eyes. Something inside her melted at the heat that flashed briefly before disappearing just as quickly. His sensual lips looked out of place on such a masculine face.

Holy cow. Her insides clenched. Her nipples poked painfully against her bra and she felt even more moisture seep from her. A quick glance at Jackson's glittering eyes had her all but crawling with need.

How the hell could she stay here with them for a year and not go crazy?

But Jackson had been right. She had no other option.

"Okay." She nodded. "I have to go home to quit my job and get the rest of my things. I can be back in a week." She would use the time away from them to put things back into perspective and push all lascivious thoughts from her mind. Shayne moved even closer toward her, shaking his head and she fought the urge to back away. "No. Call your boss from here. We'll send someone for your things. You can't go anywhere as long as there's a threat to your safety."

His deep rumbling tone weakened her knees. Samantha's gaze slid to Jackson. His cocky grin had disappeared. Now he looked at her thoughtfully, steadily, and this look unnerved her even more.

With Shayne so close, she started trembling, almost overwhelmed by her completely feminine response to his raw masculinity. She had to force herself to focus on his words as he continued.

"I don't know who these men are that threatened to hurt you but I'll find out. Until I find them, you will stay on the ranch. My men are always on the lookout for strangers. Until we pay them off, they're a threat."

Samantha nodded. "Okay. Thanks." Please just let him move away before she embarrassed herself.

Her breath caught and she felt a fresh rush of moisture as Shayne crossed his thickly roped arms over his chest, his whole demeanor dominant and unyielding. "You will not leave the ranch without either Jackson or me. Any of my men who try to take you off the ranch will be fired. If you try to leave, your brother goes back to jail."

Samantha bristled at the implication that she would run out on them and lifted her chin. "I don't welsh on my debts. I'll work as your housekeeper for the next year and make sure my brother stays out of trouble."

Shayne gripped her raised chin. Oh God. She couldn't even stand that impersonal touch. Her senses had gone on overload and she knew she couldn't take any more. She wanted those lips on hers. They moved as she stared at them. Panicking that she'd missed something, she jolted back to reality.

"No. *We* will keep your brother out of trouble. Your only job is to take care of us." His thumb ran over her bottom lip and she felt an answering pull between her legs. The pad of his thumb felt rough against her lips, and suddenly she wanted his hands on her elsewhere. Everywhere. What would it be like to be touched with hands as large and powerful as Shayne's?

He stared at her for several long seconds and she couldn't look away. She could only imagine how hot and intense lovemaking would be for a man like him. She shook with the need to find out. Involuntarily, she touched her tongue to his rough finger. Startled with herself, she jerked away. He dropped his hand suddenly as if he'd been burned. With a muffled curse, he glared at her before turning and striding abruptly out of the room.

Jackson watched his brother walk away and turned to her, smiling. He sobered and looked at her as though seeing her for the first time, even more intently than he had a few minutes ago. "Give me your address and the keys. I'll send someone for your things."

Samantha nodded. "I'll call my friend, Donna. I don't want her to call the police when she sees your men."

Jackson nodded and turned to leave but stopped and turned back when she touched his arm. "Tell your men to be careful. Those men already showed up at my apartment once and I don't want your men getting hurt."

Jackson frowned at her. "They didn't hurt you, did they?"

Samantha shook her head. "No. I went across the hall to Donna's when I saw them coming."

Jackson stared at her for several long seconds before nodding. "Don't worry about it. I know who to send. We're gonna have to talk about this later."

Chapter Two

Jackson got their new little housekeeper's keys and address and sent Doug and Walt to go pack her things and bring them back, warning them about the situation. He'd taken her upstairs and shown her which room she would be using and left her alone to look around.

Walking away from her had to be one of the hardest things he'd ever done in his life. The way she nibbled at that voluptuous bottom lip made his cock so hard, it made even walking painful.

The women he'd known had always been a lot more blatant than Samantha. Picking up a date for the first time, he'd been greeted at the door by women wearing little or nothing. He'd gone out with women who didn't even want to talk, just wanted the pleasure his cock could give them. Some had dated him just because they knew he and Shayne liked to share and they wanted a thrill. Even with all his experience, he struggled to control his response to this enticing bit of shy femininity.

With Samantha, he'd thought about sex, sure. His hands had itched to hold those enticing curves against him, knowing how soft and warm she would be.

And that scent.

Clean, fresh, not like the cloying perfume the women he dated usually wore. He usually came home reeking of it and couldn't wait to take a shower before going to bed. That had been one of the reasons he didn't spend the night with them.

But Samantha's enticing scent had made him want to get closer, to snuggle up to her, to have that scent linger on his pillow.

Damn, he was way out of his league here. Samantha Cross reminded him again just how shallow his life had become. He'd become bored with his life, unfulfilled. She reminded him of everything he'd ever wanted, all the dreams he and Shayne had talked about, and he'd only just met her.

He saddled his horse and rode out to where he knew Shayne would be.

At first, he'd ignored the signs of Samantha's arousal. He could get laid without all the emotional baggage she brought with her. But when he realized being around Shayne also aroused her, he'd watched them both closely.

Shayne had looked at Samantha in a way Jackson had never seen before. His brother watched Samantha with such intense longing, it had surprised the hell out of him. Every minute, Jackson wanted her more and more. As excited as a little boy on Christmas morning, he couldn't wait to get started.

When he first saw her get out of the car, he figured she had to be one of the girls from town. He'd begun to get tired of their back stabbing and bitchiness. None of them had been a challenge. Their cattiness and willingness to jump into bed with little or no effort on his part had begun to get on his nerves.

Samantha Cross, on the other hand, had been aroused and had fought to hide it. That had amused him. But once he heard Samantha Cross begin her story, he had been drawn to her. It sounded like she spent most of her life taking care of other people. Now, she would be taking care of him and his brother. None of the women he knew would have done that. She hadn't asked for the money. She hadn't left it up to her brother to pay his own debt. She'd taken full responsibility for the entire thing, even making sure that her brother got out of jail. Sure, she said she needed his help to pay off the debt, but she would have been the one living in fear.

She could have just as easily taken off and left the bills and her brother behind.

Her determination to fight her response to both of them had intrigued him even more. Most women wouldn't have bothered. They'd have made a play for Shayne and him and figured they could buy their way out of trouble with sex. Hell, he'd even propositioned her and she'd turned him down flat.

No, Samantha Cross appeared to be different than other women and she already captivated him. He also knew that she'd intrigued his brother. Not an easy thing to do.

Samantha seemed to have been just as taken with Shayne.

Finally spotting his brother, he sobered. Shayne hadn't been so lucky with women. His older brother had always been big, but once he'd hit his teens, he'd gotten *really* big. Their parents' deaths had instantly made Shayne the man of the house and he'd taken that position very seriously. He'd become hard and arrogant almost overnight. He had to in order to earn the respect of the ranch hands. He worked his ass off to keep the ranch afloat and gotten muscular and even bigger. And even more of a loner.

Shayne had never been a good looking man, and had never cared. But he told Jackson years ago that he felt too big and clumsy with women, which did bother him. Between that and his less than average looks, Shayne had pretty much given up on the fairer sex.

Until they'd begun sharing.

They both enjoyed sex more when they shared a woman. Shayne also felt more comfortable, knowing Jackson would be there and would warn him if he got too rough. The women they'd shared had been turned on by Shayne's take charge attitude in the bedroom, but Shayne wouldn't believe it.

Jackson knew his brother would never hurt a woman, but Shayne always feared he would. Especially after the rumors started.

Most women wanted a pretty face and so Jackson had gotten most of the action. Shayne had always been too busy with ranch work but he had gone out with a few of the women in town. Their not so subtle references to his wealth had turned him off until even the frequency of those dates dwindled to nothing. To save face, those bitches had quickly spread the word that Shayne was rough and crude and that's why *they* had been the ones to break it off.

Hell hath no fury and all that.

Shayne had shrugged off the comments but Jackson knew his brother well. The seed of doubt that had already been planted continued to grow. He'd walked away from women and had worked his ass off, so Jackson had food in his belly, and had done Jackson's chores in order to give Jackson time to play.

Shayne's back stiffened as Jackson approached. "What the hell are you thinking?"

Jackson hid a grin. "What are you talking about? Didn't you just tell me yesterday that we had to find a new housekeeper?" Most men shook in their boots at Shayne's glare but he'd long ago become immune.

"She's not the type of girl you're used to. She's not hard like the others and I don't want you hurting her. Besides, I don't want to lose another housekeeper."

"You're right, she's not the kind of woman I'm used to. And you don't give a damn about losing another housekeeper. I won't hurt her. But I think little Samantha got aroused around both of us and it scared the hell out of her. She tried hard not to show it."

"Bullshit," Shayne growled. "Her nipples were hard before she came into the study. Once she got a good look at me she was ready to bolt."

"That's true," Jackson nodded and shifted in his saddle to watch one of the ranch hands chase down a calf. "But it wasn't because she was scared of you. I think she got turned on by both of us and it freaked her out. She doesn't look like she's used to that kind of thing."

"Bullshit."

Jackson rode beside his brother. "We have to do something about your vocabulary."

"Fuck you."

Jackson chuckled. "Better."

They rode in silence for several minutes before Shayne sighed, a look of sad loneliness in his eyes. "Can you imagine how much damage a man like me could do to a little thing like that?" He turned away, watching the men work.

"Just because you can hurt someone doesn't mean you will. The women that spread those rumors only did it for revenge and you know it. But I don't want anyone around that would make you feel uncomfortable in your own house. I guess the best thing to do is to get rid of her. Those men probably won't do anything to her."

Shayne whipped around, his eyes glittering dangerously. "No! Are you crazy? Right now the ranch is the only place where she'll be safe. She's got enough to worry about without looking over her shoulder."

Jackson bit the inside of his mouth to keep from grinning. Yep, Shayne had already started to fall for her. He just hoped their new little housekeeper didn't hurt him. If she did, he'd get rid of her in a hurry, no matter what Shayne said.

* * * *

When Doug and Walt returned with boxes loaded with Samantha's things, Jackson opened the front door for them. "Just leave them here. We'll take them up later."

Even though he knew Samantha was in the kitchen, he didn't want the other men in her bedroom.

Since when had he ever cared about something like that?

"Boss, there's something we gotta tell ya."

Both men shifted their feet and looked more than a little pissed off.

"What is it? What happened?"

Doug, the older of the two, glanced toward the kitchen where they could hear Samantha moving around. "Maybe it would be better if we talked in private."

Uneasy now, Jackson gestured toward the study. "We'll talk in there."

Walking into the study, Jackson cursed under his breath, unaware that Shayne was in there. He gave his brother an apologetic looked that Shayne waved away.

"I said no. I don't want you people digging up my ranch. Stop calling. Stop sending letters. No more emails."

Despite Shayne's cool tone, Jackson could see the fury on his brother's face.

Shayne gestured for the ranch hands to sit down as his face tightened even more. "If you set one foot on my land, I'll kick your ass."

Shayne disconnected, tossing the phone onto the desk and scrubbing a hand over his face before lifting a brow at Jackson. "What's up?"

Jackson took a seat in front of the desk. "Doug and Walt have something to tell us." He turned to the men. "What happened?"

Doug's lips thinned. "When we got to Miss Cross's apartment, we found this." He pulled out a knife and handed it over to Jackson. "Somebody stabbed her pillow with it. They also wrote on her mirror. 'We'll be back'."

Jackson tossed the knife onto the desk and rushed to the door. Opening it, he heard Samantha moving around the kitchen and let out a breath he hadn't realized he'd been holding.

He nodded to Shayne, who looked like he'd been kicked in the gut. "She's okay."

Walt leaned forward, his arms braced on his knees. "Her neighbor said the furniture went with the apartment. We packed everything else. She also told us that two men showed up. The first time they wrote on the mirror. They must have used the knife when they came back because the woman said it wasn't there before."

Jackson scrubbed a hand over his face. His gaze kept straying to the knife on the desk. He broke out in a cold sweat, imagining someone using that on Samantha.

"What about the neighbor? She's Samantha's friend. I don't want her hurt." The ice in Shayne's voice was unmistakable.

"She lives alone," Doug replied. "She seems like a nice girl."

Jackson swore. "If those men find out she's Samantha's friend, they could hurt her to find out where she is."

Shayne picked up the phone. "I'll get Cal on it."

Jackson walked the ranch hands out as Shayne spoke to the security consultant. "Thanks, guys. Tell the others to keep an eye out. No strangers on the property. None."

* * * *

A few days later, Samantha and the men had settled into a routine. She'd also started making headway in giving the big house a good cleaning. She had already rearranged the kitchen so she could find everything.

Although she kept busy, she still had way too much time to think. She'd spoken to Donna, who now had a bodyguard courtesy of Shayne and Jackson.

They'd brushed off her thanks, telling her again to stay on the ranch.

"I mean it, Samantha," Shayne had warned. "You do not leave the ranch alone."

Shayne and Jackson had dropped the charges against her brother and after agreeing to their terms, Petey had come back to work. He moved back into the bunkhouse, staying with several of the other men. She didn't know what Shayne and Jackson had said to her brother, but Petey seemed subdued.

The day after she'd arrived, she saw him in the yard and popped out to talk to him. She'd been so worried that the men would get to him before Shayne and Jackson could pay them off.

Petey brushed off her concern. "Don't worry about it, sis. You fixed everything. Again."

Tears had stung her eyes as she'd watched him walk away. Mad at herself for letting him get to her, she'd walked back inside.

Although she checked for him in the yard, she hadn't gone out to speak to him since.

A quick peek in the oven told her that the chicken was done, but so far neither Shayne nor Jackson had come in to eat. She glanced at the clock. They'd told her this morning they'd be in about this time. She didn't want the chicken to dry out, so she turned off the oven and went outside in search of them. Bracing herself against the wild hunger that hit her hard whenever she saw them, she walked across the yard.

Seeing several of the ranch hands gathered at the fence, she started over. There appeared to be something exciting going on. They yelled and shouted encouragement but blocked her view of whatever inspired all the commotion. She saw Petey and moved toward him. "What's going on?"

Petey turned and pulled her to stand in front of him. "Shayne's breaking a new stallion. This one's a mean one, too."

Samantha got jostled and Petey lifted her to the top rail of the fence so she could see better. What she saw stole her breath. Shayne's face looked harder than ever, a study of fierce concentration as he handled the stallion. The horse tried its best to throw him off, but Shayne didn't appear to be going anywhere.

The sounds the horse made sent a chill down her spine. It turned and twisted, bucking violently and still Shayne held on. Hard arms came around her waist, and when a jolt of awareness shot through her, she knew it had to be Jackson.

"That horse is going to kill him," she told him fearfully.

He chuckled as he lifted her from the fence. "No, Sam. Shayne does this all the time. We both do, but Shayne's better at it and takes the really mean ones. He's never been thrown."

Samantha tried to ignore the heat at her back as she continued to watch Shayne. The horse appeared to be tiring and then all of a sudden started bucking again. Shayne held on, his gloved hands tight on the reins and she could see how his muscles bunched and shifted, pitting his brute strength and determination against the horse's intent to throw him off.

She couldn't take her eyes off of him, fear for him warring with the thrill she got watching him. All that hard packed muscle drew her attention in a way she knew should embarrass her, but right now she couldn't tear her eyes away. The hard chest heating her back drew just as much of her attention, sending her heart racing. She tried to move away, but with the fence in front of her, she didn't have anywhere to go.

Jackson's arm went around her waist, pulling her back against him. "Back up, Sam. I took you off the fence because I don't want you to get hurt."

The deep voice next to her ear made her shudder.

"I'm going to have to talk to your brother. I don't want you in that kind of danger again. If that horse had managed to get close to the fence, your legs could have been crushed."

She nodded, startled when his hands moved to her hips. Keeping her eyes forward, she watched as the horse apparently gave up. The ranch hands applauded loudly as Shayne led the horse toward the stable.

Samantha drew a breath. "It appears that Shayne won."

Jackson turned her to face him. The other men moved away, heading for Shayne until the two of them stood alone. "With a little determination, a gentle approach and a firm hand, just about anything can be tamed."

Why comments like that soaked her panties, Samantha had no idea, but Jackson apparently did, because he said things like that to her with increasing regularity.

Lifting her chin, she fought her reaction to his provocative statement. "I just came out to tell you both that lunch is ready."

She swept past him and started back toward the house, ignoring his laugh. Damn it. He knew damned well what he did to her.

* * * *

She'd just taken the chicken out of the oven when she heard the door to the laundry room open. The men had finally come in for lunch. She knew they'd take off their hats and boots before coming into the kitchen to wash their hands.

Her attraction to them had grown daily and it had become increasingly hard to hide it. Jackson's coolness toward her on that first day had changed dramatically. He touched her often, brushing against her as he walked by, a hand on her waist as he looked over her shoulder to see what she had cooked.

And he kept making those ridiculous comments, like the one he'd made at the fence, his eyes full of promise and intention.

Shayne on the other hand, spoke to her only when necessary and appeared to do his best to ignore her. He watched her constantly, however, his gaze intent whenever he looked at her. She became clumsy and flustered around both of them and it only seemed to get worse every day.

She just had to pay her debt and she could go. She had to remember that.

She hurriedly put the food on the table, knowing from experience just how hungry they'd be.

Jackson smiled at her as he walked in. "Smells good, Sam." He leaned over her as she got the rest of the food from the counter. He reached around her for the potatoes and bread, keeping his arms there for longer than necessary before moving away to carry them to the table.

Another one of those slick moves that beaded her nipples and had her stomach clenching. Damn. She wished he would stop that. She had no idea how she would last a year this way. "Thanks. I hope you guys like it."

She turned to find Shayne's eyes on her.

He nodded and looked away. "It's fine."

Frowning at him, she poured them each a glass of the iced tea she'd made earlier and sat down to join them. The first night she'd made dinner, she hadn't sat down with them. Not sure of her place, she'd served them and gone up to her room to unpack. Shayne had come to her room and hauled her out to the kitchen without a word and plopped her in her chair. She'd eaten with them ever since. "Petey said that the men he owes money to are meeting him Saturday night to pick it up."

Shayne served her a chicken breast before serving himself and she found herself touched at yet another of his thoughtful gestures. "Yeah."

His eyes narrowed as he looked at her and he got up without a word. He reached into the refrigerator, coming back to the table with the carton of milk. He looked pointedly at where she absently rubbed her stomach and filled her glass before seating himself again.

He kept doing things like that, reinforcing her certainty that he never missed a thing. Every time the subject of those thugs Petey owed money to arose, her stomach burned. And every time, he got her a glass of milk without saying a word.

When she smiled and thanked him, he just grunted and looked away.

Jackson spooned potatoes onto her plate, grinning at her. "If you keep cooking the way you do, we might just keep you forever. Right, Shayne?"

Samantha snuck a glance at Shayne who just glared at Jackson and shoved another forkful of potatoes into his mouth. "Speaking of food, I've got to get some. I don't even have anything for dinner tomorrow."

When Jackson didn't respond, Shayne glared at him again and mumbled. "Jackson can take you to the store tomorrow morning."

Although he did things like getting milk for her, he'd avoided spending one minute more with her than he had to and had been very careful not to touch her. The mixed messages drove her crazy.

"I'm not contagious, you know! *You* could have offered to take me to town."

Shayne raised a brow at her outburst. Even Jackson blinked at her. Surprised at herself, she snapped her mouth closed. What the hell was wrong with her? Being aroused for the better part of a week had obviously affected her brain. She opened her mouth to apologize when Shayne spoke.

"I don't go to town unless I have to. Eat your lunch."

Samantha hated his cold indifference and wanted to provoke some kind of reaction from him but feared the consequences. She settled for glaring at him. When he stared back at her stonily, it only pissed her off more. Taking a deep breath, she fought down her anger. She really wanted to get along with both of them and live in peace. She just had to ignore the way they made her feel, the riot of emotions they created in her.

It scared her that it had become more than physical. Much more. She knew damned well that men like Shayne and Jackson could never be happy with someone like her, so she tried her best to ignore her feelings.

She saw the women who came around almost daily. She'd watched out the upstairs window as the women followed Jackson around, vying for his attention. They all looked so beautiful and sophisticated. When she saw the way Shayne glared at any that had the nerve to approach him, she knew he could never be interested in her. Next to those women, she felt plain and unattractive.

She couldn't help how she felt, though, and struggled to come up with something to say. "That was really good, what you did with that horse out there."

Shayne nodded and continued eating.

Tense as hell and hurt at being ignored, she snapped. "You could say thank you."

Shayne raised a brow. "For what?"

"I gave you a compliment."

Shayne looked at Jackson, obviously confused. Jackson just grinned before shoving more food into his mouth. Shayne glared at him and looked back at her, still frowning. "It's my job. I shouldn't be complimented for it. It has to be done, so I do it."

"It's nice to get a compliment. Like when Jackson says that he likes my cooking. That's my job, too. But it's nice to hear someone say I cooked something they liked."

Shayne frowned at her. "I eat it, don't I?"

Samantha sighed inwardly. Why had she even started this? "Well, it's just polite."

"I'm not polite. If you want polite, you're going to have to talk to Jackson." He threw down his fork and stood, clearly intending to storm out of the kitchen.

Samantha jumped to her feet. With a hand on his arm, she rushed to stand in front of him before he could leave. Damn it. What had she done? "I'm sorry, Shayne. I didn't mean that you're not polite. You've been very sweet to me."

"Sweet?" His eyes narrowed. "Now you're making fun of me."

He really didn't like her at all. She smiled sadly. "No. I'm not."

Shayne crossed his arms over his chest, raising a brow sarcastically. "Okay, how am I *sweet*?"

Wishing she'd never started any of this, Samantha shrugged and pointed at her plate. "Like when you gave me the chicken breast because you remembered I like it. Like when you get me a glass of milk when my stomach burns. I just wanted to tell you how impressed I was with what you did with that horse and I felt like you were trying to blow me off. It hurt."

Shayne watched her through narrowed eyes. "Sit down, Samantha."

She sat back down, watching him through her lashes as he took his own seat and picked up his fork. He paused, not looking at her.

"I'm not good with stuff like that. Jackson's the polite one. Don't take it personally." He turned his attention back to his plate and starting eating again, apparently finished with the conversation.

When she looked at Jackson, she found him smiling at her as he looked back and forth between her and his brother. He winked, grinned and continued eating his lunch.

What the hell was that all about? She picked up her own fork, watching both of them. When they started talking about cattle, she let her mind drift.

Shayne's sensitivity about not being as polished as Jackson pulled at her. He kept everything to himself, never showing anything of what he was thinking or feeling. Except for the way his eyes glittered sometimes when she caught him unaware, he seemed completely cold. Because of the way he kept himself closed off, she had no idea what those looks meant.

As soon as Shayne finished eating, he got up from the table and left without a word.

Samantha watched him go, staring at the empty doorway, listening to the sounds of him putting on his boots and going out the back door. Turning back to her plate, she pushed her food around, all appetite gone.

"Don't let Shayne get to you, honey. He's fighting himself. He's trying very hard to ignore you."

Samantha picked up her plate to scrape the uneaten food into the garbage can. "He's doing a good job."

Jackson chuckled. "No, he's not. You should have seen the way he lit into your brother for putting you on the fence."

Dropping her plate into the sink, Samantha spun. "He saw that?"

Jackson grinned. "Shayne knows everything that goes on at the ranch. And with you. So do I."

Samantha blinked, not sure she wanted to hear this. "I'm just the housekeeper."

"You've somehow managed to become more than that to both of us and you know it."

Samantha collected Shayne's dishes from the table and moved back to the sink. "I don't know what you're talking about. I've only known you for a few days. Shayne can't even stand to be in the same room with me and you have a never-ending line of girlfriends who show up all the time. I'll work here for a year as your housekeeper. At the end of that year, I'm leaving."

"What did your boss say when you called him?"

Samantha blinked at the sudden change of conversation and turned back to him. "He said not to come back, and that he wouldn't give me a reference because I quit without notice. Why?"

Jackson got up to pour himself a cup of coffee. "Want some?"

Samantha shook her head and went back to clearing the table.

Instead of sitting back down, Jackson leaned against the counter, watching her as she washed dishes. "If you want to leave here at the end of the year, I'll help you get another job. But I hope you'll stay."

Samantha trembled at his soft tone. She concentrated on not dropping the plates she washed as he continued to stare at her.

"Why do you let your brother walk all over you?" he asked quietly.

Samantha carefully rinsed the plate and put it in the stand to drain. "You don't know what you're talking about. Petey needs me."

"Your brother treats you like shit. He's a spoiled brat that expects you to take care of him and get him out of trouble."

"It's none of your business."

Jackson slammed his cup down on the counter with such force, she jumped, surprised it hadn't broken. "That's where you're wrong. You're our responsibility now. You live and work on our ranch and so does your brother. We're going to teach him to be a man and to stop depending on you to get him out of trouble."

"Damn it, Jackson. Stay out of it."

"Why?"

"Because."

Jackson gripped her chin. "Not good enough. You're not doing him any favors, Sam. He's just going to keep getting into trouble."

"I'm going with him when he delivers that money."

Jackson chuckled. "You know damned well he's going to try to take off with it. No, you're not going. God only knows what those men will do when he stiffs them. Shayne and I are going and you are staying here on the ranch. The ranch hands will be here so you won't be alone."

Samantha pulled out of his grip. "I'm going."

"No."

"I have to!"

Jackson grabbed her shoulders. "Why?"

"Because I promised I'd take care of him."

When the tears started to fall, she tried to hide her face but Jackson wouldn't let her.

"You promised your mother, didn't you?"

Samantha nodded, wiping her eyes. "She said he needed me."

Jackson pulled her close, wrapping his arms around her and stroking her back soothingly. "Shayne and I will take care of your brother. We'll keep him out of trouble and make him start taking responsibility for himself."

He lifted her face, wiping his thumbs over her cheeks to dry her tears. "Shayne and I need you. We need you to trust us and to give us a chance to show you how good we can be together."

Samantha's eyes fluttered closed at the first touch of his lips on hers. When his tongue traced her lips, she parted them, nearly overwhelmed by the surge of desire. When his hands covered her breasts, she moaned into his mouth. It had been a long time since she'd been touched so intimately. Starved for it, she pushed her breasts more firmly into his hands, loving the erotic friction on her nipples.

When he lifted his head, she nearly groaned. His hands continued to move on her breasts, cupping them and teasing her nipples. She wanted to feel them on her bare skin.

"You're so sweet," he drawled, looking down at her. His hand moved down to cup her mound.

She parted her legs, her breath shaky as he stroked her through the denim.

"You're wet, aren't you, Sam? Your nipples are as hard as my cock. When I finally get you naked under me, I may never let you up again."

She groaned and tried to move closer.

Jackson gripped her shoulders again and held her at arm's length, his own breathing erratic. His eyes bored into hers. "Christ, you test my control. Stop wiggling."

His hands tightened on her shoulders. "Shayne wants you every bit as much as I do. I want this to work. I'm not taking you until you and my brother both admit that the three of us together is what you want."

He jerked her back against him, covering her mouth with his again, and kissing her hard and fast. When he lifted his head, they were both breathing heavily. He didn't speak for several long seconds.

When he finally did, it came out as a growl. "You and my brother better both come to your senses soon."

Chapter Three

Samantha decided to make beef stew for dinner, something she could keep hot. She didn't want to have to look for them again and have a repeat performance of earlier.

Knowing both of them would want a shower before dinner, she knew she'd have plenty of time to cook the biscuits.

The front porch swing had already become her favorite place and she went there now. Using her bare toes, she put it in motion, the movement never failing to soothe her.

One of the ranch hands rode along the front fence, touching the brim of his hat when he saw her. Smiling at the old fashioned gesture, she waved back, once again feeling that this could be a scene from the last century.

A pickup went by, ruining the image, the driver sounding his horn and waving at the ranch hand. She hadn't met all of the men yet, but thought it might be Doug. Jackson had introduced her to him. Doug appeared to be assigned to watching out for her.

Although the threats were never far from her thoughts, seeing Doug now reminded her of the danger to both her and her brother. Donna had told her about the knife that had been plunged into her pillow, but neither Shayne nor Jackson had mentioned it.

She assumed they hadn't wanted to scare her.

Too late. She was already scared.

She just hoped that once the men got their money that would be the end of it. She shuddered to think about what could have happened if Shayne and Jackson hadn't helped them. They'd already paid off the medical bills.

She breathed deeply, loving the smells. She felt safe here. Well, at least safe from the men in the fancy suits.

Shayne and Jackson were another matter.

If she'd simply wanted them physically, she would have been able to fight it. But wanting them while caring for them more and more every day had been much more difficult.

It seemed impossible that she'd met them only days ago. She'd already come to care for them a great deal, and every time she saw them, the feelings she had for them kept getting stronger.

She just needed to know that they cared for her the same way and that she wouldn't be just someone to have sex with while she worked here.

* * * *

Shayne walked into the kitchen, frowning to find it empty. A knot formed in his stomach. He knew it wouldn't unravel until he found Samantha.

He found it hard to believe she'd only been here a few days. She'd already become part of this place, and a part of him. If anything happened to her he didn't know what he would do and it kept him on edge the entire time he was away from her.

Wishing for the hundredth time that he could be the kind of man she'd need, he started moving from room to room, looking for her.

Not finding her in the kitchen or study, he moved to the front door, knowing how much she loved to sit on the swing. She jolted when he walked out and he cursed himself for startling her. He approached slowly, not wanting to scare her any further, stopping several feet away to lean against a post. "Are you okay?"

Samantha nodded. "I'd better go start the biscuits."

Shayne had been avoiding her as much as possible and knew she wanted to get away from him, but he couldn't resist spending a few minutes with her. "Jackson won't be in for a little while. The biscuits can wait a few more minutes."

He watched as she settled back into the swing, using her bare toes to rock it back and forth. He would love to pick her up, hold her on his lap, and swing for hours.

The sight of her tiny feet with her little pink toenails made him hard as a rock.

Samantha cleared her throat. "Jackson said that you're going with Petey to pay those guys off."

Shayne nodded. "Yeah. Doug and Walt will stay behind to watch the ranch while we're gone." The thought of not being here himself to protect her made his stomach churn.

"Do you know who they are?"

"Yes."

When he didn't add anything more, Samantha sighed. "Well? Who are they?"

Shayne deliberately relaxed his hands that had tightened into fists. Thinking about those men in her apartment and what could have happened to her, enraged him. "Bad men. Men that won't get near you again. Don't worry. They can't get to you or your brother."

He didn't tell her that the men were being watched and that the sheriff, along with Cal and his men would also be there. He didn't want her to worry and would tell her when it was over.

"I'm not a child, you know. You can tell me what's going on."

Wanting to distract her, Shayne raised a brow. "Tough, are you?"

She stared at him for so long, he thought she wouldn't answer. When a slow smile curved her lips, his groin tightened painfully.

"You think I'm scared of you, don't you?"

Shayne surprised himself by grinning. "Baby, if you knew what I'm thinking right now, it would terrify you all the way to your cute little toes."

Samantha grinned. "You think my toes are cute?"

Her smile made his cock jump and he barely stifled his groan. His face burned as her question registered. Had he really said that? He shrugged, not knowing what to say.

Samantha blinked, her violet eyes wide. "Are you flirting with me?"

Shayne's face burned even hotter. "No."

His breath caught when she stood and moved close, staring up at him. The clean, fresh scent, uniquely her, had him tightening his hands into fists to keep from reaching for her. As she stood looking up at him, it reminded him again of the huge difference in their size.

Finally, she spoke. "If you don't like me, I wish you'd just say so. If you do, stop acting like a jerk."

Stunned, Shayne could only watch her as she stormed into the house.

"She didn't seem scared to me."

Shayne turned to see a grinning Jackson coming around the side of the house.

"Shut up, Jackson."

* * * *

Right after breakfast the next morning, she and Jackson climbed into his truck to ride to town for groceries. Shayne had already gone out and she watched him from the truck window as they started down the drive. The ranch hands gathered around him, looking so much smaller next to him. Yesterday, she'd seen the way they all deferred to him. Part of it, of course, had to do with him being the boss, but she could see that he worked harder than any of them and had earned their respect with his sweat, determination, and courage. She couldn't even imagine pitting herself against an animal so much bigger than she was.

Her gaze slid to Jackson as he pulled out of the driveway. Her body, always tingling with awareness at his nearness, reacted even more so to being confined in the truck with him.

Jackson turned to grin at her wickedly. "Something on your mind?"

That wicked grin of his had her stomach clenching. She said the first thing that came to mind. "Why doesn't Shayne ever go to town?"

Jackson's jaw tightened. "He just doesn't. Drop it."

"Okay. Sorry. I was just curious." She watched his hands on the wheel. They looked big and competent and she couldn't help but wonder what they would feel like stroking her. Her face burned and she hurriedly turned to look out the window.

Jackson sighed. "Sam, I'm sorry for snapping. Shayne just doesn't like to go to town if he can avoid it."

Samantha jerked her attention back to him. "I know he tries not to spend any more time with me than he has to." She rubbed at a spot on her jeans. "I shouldn't have snapped at him at lunch yesterday. He was really quiet at dinner."

Jackson reached for her hand and folded it in his. Startled, she tried to pull away but he wouldn't let her.

"Shayne is six feet eight inches tall. Growing up, he was happy to be so big because he could help my dad out a lot. It wasn't until the women in town starting talking about how rough and crude he was that he started to feel uncomfortable with his size. That's why we starting sharing women. He's afraid to be alone with one. And when we did share a woman, we found something we'd never felt before. It satisfied us in a way we'd never known."

Samantha sat there, stunned and shifted uncomfortably in her seat. "I've heard about ménages, but I've never actually met anyone who participated in them before. What did you find that that you never had before?"

Jackson chuckled. "Shayne and I found that we fed off of each other's excitement. We found that we could make a woman come over and over again and that fed our excitement even more. Then I think Shayne liked that he no longer worried about being too rough. He liked having me there. I liked having him there. We've always been close but this made us even closer." He turned to look at her sternly. "You can't tell him that I said any of this. But it looks like Shayne is starting to care for you very much."

Jackson came to a stop sign and turned to her with an expression she hadn't seen before. His eyes gentled as he stroked her fingers. "I am, too. You're the kind of woman I'd forgotten existed. I'm having a helluva time keeping my hands off of you. But I want Shayne to realize what he feels for you and accept that he can be good to you. I've never seen him look at a woman the way he looks at you. We want to share you, Sam. Make a life with you together. I don't want my brother hurt, though. He doesn't want to believe that you're attracted to him." He sighed and released her hand as he pulled out onto the road. "I just hope Shayne realizes what we can have with you soon. The waiting is killing me."

Samantha just stared at his profile, open mouthed, astonished at the flood of moisture that now soaked her panties. At the same time, her heart pounded furiously, thinking about both of them caring for her in that way. Struck dumb, she didn't know how to answer him. Several snappy comebacks went through her mind but nothing would come out of her mouth. Finally, she settled on the least explosive. "This can't happen. Shayne doesn't even like me. And besides, I'm your housekeeper, nothing more. If you expect me to pay my debt in another way, you're mistaken."

Jackson grinned. "If you had been the type to pay your debt on your back, you wouldn't still be here. But there's going to come a time, real soon, that you're going to have to be honest with yourself. Do you think that I don't see that you want both Shayne and me?"

Samantha kept staring out the window. "I don't do casual sex." *Especially with men she knew would break her heart.*

"Once again, if you did, you wouldn't still be here. Shayne and I are looking for something more from a woman."

Samantha blinked. "Oh, right, I forgot. You want to share a woman forever," she muttered sarcastically.

Jackson smiled. "Yes. We do. Kids, the whole thing, with a woman who sleeps nice and warm between us every night."

Samantha closed her eyes as the image imprinted itself in her mind. What would it be like to have Shayne and Jackson make love to her? What would it feel like to be lying cuddled between them in the dark? *Snap out of it, Sam!* "I'm not the woman you need." She tried not to squirm under Jackson's scrutiny.

"Maybe," he murmured. "Then again, maybe not. Shayne and I aren't always gentle lovers. We like to hear a woman scream her pleasure. Probably not what you're looking for, right?"

Samantha bit her lip against the wave of longing. "Right." She thought about the books she loved to read. Jackson and Shayne would be even more than the characters in the erotic romances she collected.

When they finally got to the store, she hurriedly scrambled out of the truck, needing to put some distance between them.

But of course, Jackson stayed with her as she shopped for groceries. Because of that, her shopping took much longer. She had to keep working around the women that Jackson seemed to attract in droves. They glared at her, asking Jackson about her.

She tried to move away from him several times, seething at the women's rudeness, but he stayed right with her. It appeared every woman in town between the ages of twenty and forty had decided to do their grocery shopping as soon as Jackson had walked into the store. Funny, none of them had grocery carts.

A redhead seemed to be the most intent for his attention, trying to battle a well endowed blond to get closer to him.

Amused, Samantha headed for the meats. "Jackson, do you and Shayne like pork chops?"

"Jackson does. Shayne will eat anything raw."

Samantha turned to see that the stunning redhead had managed to wrap herself around Jackson. She recognized her as one of the women who came out to the ranch and followed Jackson like a puppy. "Excuse me?"

"Jackson, you haven't introduced me to your new friend."

"Samantha, Monica. Monica, Samantha. Yeah, Sam, we like pork chops. You're such a good cook, we like whatever you make."

"Oh, is this the new housekeeper? I heard her brother got into some trouble," Monica sneered, snuggling closer to Jackson. "Have you warned her yet about your brother?"

Samantha dropped the meat into the cart.

Jackson's face tightened as he scowled at the redhead and pulled from her grasp. He looked so cold and disgusted. Samantha would want to crawl into a hole if he ever looked at her that way, but the redhead appeared oblivious.

She raised a brow at the woman. "Warn me about Shayne?"

The redhead managed to grip Jackson's arm again. "You have to be careful with Shayne. He's not sophisticated at all. Not like Jackson here." She purred and Samantha wanted to throw up. Now she had a good idea why Shayne wouldn't come to town.

Jackson extricated himself yet again from the redhead's clutches and grabbed Samantha's arm. "Come on, Sam. Let's go."

Samantha fumed and stood her ground. She absolutely did not believe what this viper had said about Shayne. Sure he was big. But that didn't mean he was some kind of an animal. She would love to get the chance—No, Sam don't go there. Shayne was probably the last person in the world that needed defending but she just couldn't help herself.

She smiled, while inside she just wanted to ram her shopping cart into the vicious redhead. "But he's soooo wild. All that raw masculinity."

A steel band wrapped around her waist as Jackson pulled her back against him. He growled in her ear loud enough for the women to hear. "Come on, honey. Let's finish the shopping. I need to get the hell out of here."

Samantha knew her nipples had beaded and poked at the front of her shirt. Being held against Jackson's hard body put her system on overload. *Not good, Sam.*

Her eyes slid to Monica, pleased to see that the other woman did not look at all happy to see Jackson's hands on her. Her friends that had gathered around her began to snicker at her while watching Jackson nervously.

Monica finally recovered. The jealousy and anger showed clearly as her eyes shot daggers at her. "Jackson, what's going on?"

The hand on her hip felt hot through her jeans as he patted her. "Sam, go finish the shopping. I'll be right there."

Monica looked like a landed fish the way she kept opening and closing her mouth with nothing coming out.

Samantha started to push the cart, stopping again several feet away, watching out of the corner of her eye as the blond sidled up to Jackson. "Jackson, I thought we had an understanding. I'd love to fuck you and Shayne together."

Samantha moved away a little further and began picking out chicken, making sure she could still eavesdrop without appearing to. Still trying to come to terms with the erotic pleasure she'd gotten from Jackson's touch, she continued to pick up items haphazardly, not really seeing them.

The way Monica had spoken about Shayne had enraged her. Even though Jackson had already told her about the rumors, it still surprised the hell out of her.

The blond ran her hands over Jackson's chest and Samantha bit her lip again to keep from screaming at her not to touch him. *None of your business, Sam.*

Samantha watched as Jackson pulled her hands away from his chest and chuckled. "You're the one who told everyone that Shayne was rough and crude. If he didn't please you before why would you want him to fuck you again?"

Blondie shrugged. "We never actually had sex, but—"

"He knew you were more interested in his money than in him. He hated it and your cattiness, so he dumped you. That's why you started saying things about him. Now you're trying to tell me that you want a shot at both of us?" Jackson asked sarcastically and loudly enough for everyone around them to hear.

The blond turned a deep red when she saw they had an audience. "Well, he just seemed so rough, but if he's rough in a good way, maybe we can have some fun."

Samantha heard Jackson's answering laugh and she rolled her cart away, unable to listen to anymore. She didn't care whom Jackson had sex with. Or Shayne for that matter.

With Jackson no longer in sight, she could finally concentrate on her shopping. She needed spices. Whoever had done the cooking previously had apparently used only salt, pepper and cinnamon.

Samantha needed more. Once she found them, she looked them over, mentally planning this week's meals. With recipes running through her head, she selected a few. Lost in her thoughts, she nearly jumped out of her skin when someone touched her shoulder.

"Miss, can I have a word with you?"

She gasped and spun, her hand over her thudding heart, to find a large man standing there and staring at her in a way that sent chills up her spine. Taller than Jackson, he looked heavily muscled.

He smiled apologetically. "I'm sorry I startled you."

Although not as handsome as Jackson, he had a killer smile, but some instinct made her uncomfortable around him. His eyes had the same cold look of the men who had broken into her apartment. Her stomach clenched in fear when she saw that this man also wore a suit. She couldn't help glancing around for Jackson. Not seeing him, she dumped the spices in the cart and moved around it, making sure it stood between her and the stranger, all the while cursing her fear.

Would she spend the rest of her life afraid of men in suits? "What do you want to talk to me about?"

"My name is Bruce Graham. I need to speak with Mr. Montgomery, but I can't get on the ranch. I heard you work there. I was hoping you could give him a message for me."

"Jackson Montgomery is here with me. I'll go get him."

When she started to move away, he put a hand on her arm to stop her. "No, not Jackson. I need to speak with Shayne Montgomery. Will you give him my card and tell him it's of vital importance that he call me as soon as possible?"

Samantha pulled away, repulsed by his touch. She couldn't find any fault with his behavior but for some reason he made her uneasy. She took the proffered card and moved away. "Sure, I'll give it to him."

She started to walk away and again he stopped her, gripping her forearm.

"Don't touch me!"

Although he raised his hands in surrender, his eyes flashed angrily before he shuttered them again. He smiled, all traces of anger gone, making her wonder if she'd imagined it.

"I'm sorry. I don't mean to scare you, but this is very important. The Dakota Ranch has oil on it, enough to make Shayne and Jackson Montgomery very rich men."

"I'll tell them and give Shayne your card." She just wanted to get away from him.

"Tell Shayne to call me. It's very important that he calls me before it's too late."

Samantha pushed the card into the back pocket of her jeans. "I told you I would."

The anger flared in his eyes again before it was quickly extinguished. "Don't forget." He ran a finger down her cheek, making her flinch. "Until we meet again."

Samantha jerked away from him and practically ran down the aisle towards the front of the store.

Finally she got to the checkout, where Jackson joined her to pay for the groceries, grinning, and with the women still trailing him. They actually followed him out to his truck. Unbelievable.

Ignoring the women trailing Jackson and vying for his attention, Samantha kept glancing around for the man in the suit.

She got into the passenger seat and left Jackson to deal with loading the groceries. She searched the parking lot, but saw no sign of the man who'd been in the store. Angry at herself for being afraid of him, she threw her purse to the floor. What could he have done to her with a store full of people there?

Jackson got in the truck, still grinning, and she looked over to see the redhead and the blond glaring at her as they said their goodbyes to Jackson. Forgetting about the man in the store, she glared back at them.

Riding back to the ranch, Samantha crossed her arms over her chest and stared stonily out the windshield. Just because she didn't care who Jackson slept with didn't mean that she had to put up with women fawning all over him in the grocery store, did it? It had ended up taking her twice as long to shop as it should have. He'd wasted her time. So had the man who'd given her the card. What was his name? Bruce Graham, yeah, that's it.

She had plenty of things to do back at the ranch and now she would be behind. She wanted to hit something.

What kind of barracudas lived in this town? Following Jackson like that and talking about Shayne. They didn't even know him. Sure he was big, but he'd been gentle and kind to her.

Oh, but what would it feel like to be the center of his attention, to have that big body and raw masculinity focused on her? It seemed impossible that she'd finally met men, real men, the kind that she'd fantasized about for years, and would never have them. *Whoa! Sam, those are only fantasies.*

Damn it.

She glanced at Jackson to see that he looked very pleased with himself. Why not? The women crawled all over him. She didn't care. He'd pissed her off by making her late getting home to do her chores. And what about the way he'd wrapped himself around her in front of everybody? How dare he? That's what put those crazy ideas in her head, arousing her. Just thinking about it got her hot again. All of this was Jackson's fault. He made her feel things that she knew she shouldn't feel and filled her with a need that she knew would remain unfulfilled. Bastard.

Samantha stormed into the house, leaving Jackson to carry in the groceries. She found Shayne sitting at the kitchen table drinking a glass of iced tea.

"It's about damned time."

Samantha whirled on him. "Don't blame me! Blame Casanova out there!"

Shayne nodded and stood. "Monica and the others follow him around like puppies?"

"Yeah, and some blond bimbo named Tracy. It took me twice as long to shop."

Shayne actually blanched when she'd mentioned Tracy and she could have bitten her tongue. Jackson walked in, dropped several bags on the table, grinned at her and walked back out again. Shayne turned to go out to the truck. "I'll go help with the groceries."

"Wait."

When he stopped and turned to her, she dug the card out of her pocket and handed it to him. "A man stopped me at the store and told me to give this to you. He said to tell you there's oil on the ranch and he wants you to call him."

Shayne's face turned to stone. "He talked to you?"

Samantha nodded, unnerved at both his expression and tone. "Yes, in the store."

He moved fast, grabbing her by the waist and lifting her a good foot off the floor. "Stay away from that man," he told her through clenched teeth.

Samantha blinked. "But I—"

His eyes blazed as he pulled her so close their faces nearly touched. "You stay the fuck away from him. Don't disobey me on this, Samantha. You'll regret it."

He put her down, turning away abruptly and stormed out of the kitchen. He went out to the truck, marching up to Jackson.

She heard a heated discussion but couldn't make out the words. She touched her waist, where the heat from his hands still lingered. Even as mad as he'd been, she hadn't been afraid that he'd hurt her.

Please don't let me fall in love with him!

Very afraid that it might already be too late, she slowly began to put away the groceries.

* * * *

Jackson did most of the talking during lunch, happy and grinning and she just wanted to smack him. After she'd eaten, she stood and started cleaning up, slamming the cabinet drawers in frustration.

Finally, Jackson drawled. "If you slam one more drawer, I'm turning you over my knee and paddling your ass."

Samantha froze with her hand on the drawer she'd been about to slam. Her pulse raced and she closed her eyes against the wave of pure lust that washed over her. Why the hell had the threat of a spanking in that low tone created such need? Keeping her face carefully blank, she turned to face him. "You wouldn't dare."

Shayne looked equally startled and looked over at her. Her breath caught at the heat in his eyes. When those hot eyes ran over her body, lingering on her breasts, it took every ounce of self control she possessed not to cover them with her hands.

Jackson leaned back in his chair and stared back at her, his eyes flicking to her breasts. "Slam one more drawer and find out."

Shayne bit off something under his breath and stood, moving to stand in front of her. Without warning, he lifted her onto the counter, and leaned down until his eyes were level with hers. His shoulders blocked out the rest of the room as he loomed over her.

Swallowing painfully, she stared at him, wondering what he would do. She forced herself to remain still as he reached out a thick finger to trace her cheek. She burned where he touched her. Her nipples tightened painfully and her pussy clenched, weeping desperately.

Her breath caught as his finger traced down her cheek and moved over her bottom lip. His gaze followed the track of his caress, seemingly mesmerized.

Gripping the edge of the countertop, her chest burned and she suddenly realized she'd been holding her breath. It came out in a shudder when Shayne's finger moved back and forth over her lips before sliding down to her chin and beneath it. Applying pressure, he lifted it until her eyes met his. Caught in his heavy lidded gaze, she could do nothing but stare at him.

Oh God, she wanted him so much.

She couldn't prevent a gasp as the pad of his thumb touched her bottom lip, pressing down to force her lips open.

His face tightened and he released her so abruptly, she almost fell. He caught her and settled her back on the counter and with a glare at Jackson, turned and walked out. She heard the sounds of him pulling on his boots, and a few seconds later the back door slammed.

Stunned, she sat there, trying to make sense of what had just happened, so aroused she could hardly catch her breath.

Jackson got up and started toward her. The look on his face and the way his eyes had darkened made him look far too dangerous. With her senses spiraling out of control, she gulped as he moved closer, that wide chest coming nearer with each step.

He leaned over her as Shayne had just done and lightly rubbed his lips over hers. When he traced them with his tongue, her lips parted automatically. Smiling, he straightened. He startled the hell out of her when he stroked her nipples where they poked out at the front of her shirt. "Your time is running out, baby."

She tightened her thighs against the erotic pull at her slit.

He smiled at her, tracing her cheek as Shayne had and with a last tender look, turned to follow his brother.

Sitting on the counter, trembling with need and emotion, she poked out her tongue to touch the spot Jackson's tongue had just stroked.

She had to harden her heart against them before they destroyed her.

First, she had to get her body under control.

She'd never last the year.

Chapter Four

Samantha finished cleaning up from lunch, not slamming any more drawers.

Something about Jackson had changed and it excited and scared the hell out of her. He'd already told her that he meant to have her but she didn't know if she could handle it. She had an idea what his 'time is running out' meant.

But being involved with two men was a fantasy, something out of her books. Nobody really lived that way and she didn't know if she even had the courage to try. Her heart had become involved. Even attempting it could break her.

She had plenty of time before she had to put the roast and potatoes in the oven. She just had to make some fresh iced tea. Oh no. She suddenly remembered that she'd forgotten to buy coffee at the grocery store. She'd used the last of it for breakfast this morning. Jackson's floozies and that man had distracted her and made her forget it. Damn.

She knew they'd both want coffee after dinner but even if they could go without it then, they'd all definitely want some tomorrow morning.

She went to the window not seeing either of them, and wondered what she should do. Shayne had warned her about not leaving the ranch. But if they were going to meet with the men Petey owed money to Saturday night, going out shouldn't be a problem. They'd have no reason to hurt her now. She would be fine just running to the store for coffee and would be back before either one of them even knew she'd been gone.

Slipping her sandals back on, she grabbed her purse and keys and headed out the door.

Once at the store, it didn't take long to find the coffee, especially with no one around to block her way. The next time she came to the grocery store she would definitely come alone.

After rushing through the checkout, she raced to her car, coming to an abrupt halt when she saw Bruce Graham leaning against it.

Forcing herself to move closer, she nevertheless stopped several feet away. "What do you want?"

Anger flashed in his eyes. "Don't get high and mighty with me. You're just a housekeeper who keeps her job by fucking her employers."

"Kiss my ass," Samantha snapped. "Get away from my car."

"Did you give Shayne my message?"

"Yes, now go away."

His smile sent a chill down her spine. "Tell him you saw me."

Samantha watched as he straightened and walked away. Why would he want her to tell Shayne that she saw him?

Yeah, like she would tell him. She wasn't even supposed to be here. Damn, she had to get back home before they found out she'd gone.

She hurried back to the ranch, finally turning into the long driveway and carefully parking her car exactly where it had been before. Turning off the engine, she heard a slam and looked up to see both Shayne and Jackson coming down the porch steps and heading straight for her.

Uh oh. They both looked livid. Damn.

Shayne yanked open her car door, making her wince as the door hinges groaned. She rushed to explain. "It's Jackson's fault. With all his girlfriends around I forgot to get the—Hey! What are you doing?"

He'd pulled her out of the car and tossed her over his shoulder, heading back into the house with Jackson on his heels.

"The coffee!"

"Fuck the coffee!" Shayne growled and strode to the kitchen. He dropped her to her feet, grabbed her by the shoulders and shook her. "You scared the hell out of me! Didn't I tell you not to leave the ranch?"

Shayne in a rage was a sight to behold. His already hard features had tightened even more. His eyes looked blacker than ever. She had to get him calmed down. Hoping to soften him up, she smiled and laid a hand on his chest, trying to ignore the heat and the play of hard muscle under her hand. He looked madder than hell. "I just ran out to get coffee. I forgot it earlier. Nothing happened. I figured that since you've already arranged to pay those men, they have no reason to hurt me. I thought I'd be back before you even noticed I was gone."

"So you thought you'd be back before I found out about it? You figured I would never know that you'd disobeyed me?" Shayne's dangerously soft voice gave her a strange feeling in the pit of her stomach. She recognized part of it as fear, but that glittering look in his eyes made her feel something more. She'd never seen him like this before. All the cold remoteness he'd shown her had disappeared. There was no doubt in her mind that she had his undivided attention and it scared the hell out of her.

"Shayne, I just wanted to—"

"I don't give a damn what you wanted to do. I ought to pull those jeans off of you and give you the bare ass spanking you deserve! This is my ranch and everyone on it obeys my orders or pays the consequences. For you that would be a red ass. Didn't I tell you that you're not allowed to leave the ranch unless you're with either me or Jackson?"

"Yes, but—"

"Did anyone stop you?"

"Why would anyone stop me?"

Shayne's eyes darkened even more. "That's not an answer. And if you lie to me, I'll know it. I swear I'll put you over my knee. Now, did anyone stop you?"

Damn. Not knowing if he could really tell if she lied or not, she opted for the truth. "Bruce Graham was waiting for me by my car."

"Fuck! I told you to stay away from him. He's bad news, Samantha. Didn't I tell you to stay on the fucking ranch?"

Samantha's eyes slid to Jackson who somehow managed to look fierce and smug at the same time.

Shayne grabbed her chin and forced her to face him, leaning down close. His eyes looked anything but cold now. "Jackson can't help you. You're dealing with me now. You scared me to death. If anything had happened to you—Damn you, Samantha."

Before she could blink, his mouth covered hers. He lifted her and her legs wrapped around his waist automatically as she struggled to get closer. His kiss meant to punish, bruising her lips as he took her mouth, forcing his tongue inside.

He kissed her ruthlessly, stealing her breath as he all but devoured her. His huge arms tightened around her as he groaned. Between one heartbeat and the next, his mouth gentled.

Wrapped in his embrace, she clung to him, her hands tangling in his hair to hold him close. His hand cupped the back of her head, his hands caressing her hair as he held her in place. Everywhere he touched, she could feel his heat and her mind and body spun out of control. Plastered against him, with his arms wrapped around her, she felt him everywhere.

She'd never felt so needed, or so desired as she did at that moment. Completely wrapped around each other, she still struggled to get closer. She knew he could crush her easily, but the hands that held her firmly in place stroked her gently.

The combination went to her head and she couldn't have stopped if her life depended on it. Her body flared to life, needing him to fulfill her.

Desperate groans bubbled up from deep in her throat. She thought of nothing else but him and the raging inferno he'd started inside her. She rubbed herself against him, trying to ease the lust that grew even stronger. Her nipples beaded painfully, needing to be stroked. Her pussy wept with need, clenching uselessly, begging to be filled.

His chest, hard and hot, burned her. Her nipples and slit, forced hard against him, burned even hotter. Even in his tight embrace, she couldn't stay still. Grinding herself against him, she whimpered in frustration that she couldn't get closer.

His big hand covered her bottom and pulled her more firmly against him, giving her more of the friction her body craved. Her clit throbbed, feeling twice its normal size, burning as he tilted her against him with the hand on her bottom. She screamed into his mouth as wave after wave of blinding pleasure washed over her. Her whole body stiffened as it continued, as every nerve ending exploded in almost painful pleasure. Never had she felt such absolute bliss. She'd never dreamed pleasure like this existed. It touched her everywhere, filled her completely.

She panicked as it consumed her and began to struggle. Shayne lifted his mouth from hers and held her cheek against his, his deep voice crooning in her ear. "I've got you, baby. Let go."

Held against him this way, she had no choice. When the burst began to diminish, Shayne lifted his head to stare down at her, his eyes full of heat and astonishment. "You came."

Samantha's face burned and she ducked her head, slumping against him.

With a hand on her bottom still holding her up, he used the other to lift her chin. "No. Don't hide from me, baby."

She looked up at him through her lashes to find him watching her, his eyes filled with wonder. She'd never heard that soft tone in his voice before. It warmed her, filled her with joy that he would let his guard down, even a little, with her. Reaching up, she cupped his cheek. When he turned his face into her caress and kissed her palm, her heart melted as her insides fluttered to life again.

He rubbed his thumb over her bottom lip and she shuddered, astonished to realize he held her with only one arm. "You're not afraid of me?"

She shook her head. "No. Yes." She looked over at Jackson. She'd forgotten he was in the room. "I don't know what you want from me. I don't do things like this. Please don't play games with me."

Shayne brushed away a tear she hadn't known she'd shed and set her down on the counter, keeping her legs spread by standing between them. "I don't play games."

Samantha's gaze slid to Jackson when he moved closer, his expression much the same as his brother's. "He said that you sh-share women."

Shayne smiled at her tenderly, a look she'd never seen on his face before. "We do. But with you, it's not a game. Do you want both of us, Samantha?"

Samantha looked at each of them and nodded slowly, afraid of what she was admitting, afraid of the way they made her feel, afraid that she would hurt one of them by admitting that she wanted both of them. Being shared by two men was so far out of her experience, she didn't know if she could handle it.

Shayne lifted her chin, his eyes still tender. "You really came. I haven't even touched you intimately yet."

Samantha's face burned, but he wouldn't let her look away.

"I want to touch more of you. I think Jackson does, too. Give me those lips again."

When Shayne lowered his mouth to hers again, her eyes fluttered closed on a groan. This time he didn't lift her against him. Instead he reached for the buttons of her shirt. While Shayne worked at her shirt, Jackson stroked her. One hand ran through her hair while the other touched what Shayne revealed. Shayne's mouth gentled on hers, stroking and nibbling her sensitive lips. When he lifted his head, she whimpered in her throat and tried to follow him.

"I'll give you more, baby. First let us see you."

Jackson unhooked her bra, baring her breasts to their gazes. The look in their eyes excited her even more. Both men wore similar looks of need, their faces tight. Each reached tentatively for a breast, as if waiting for her to change her mind.

She had already gone well past that.

Her body screamed for relief, yearned to be touched, stroked. As they moved close, she couldn't help but arch toward them, gasping at the first feel of their rough hands on her ultra sensitive breasts. For both of them to be touching her this way drove all doubts from her mind. They touched her reverently, their fingers moving over her slowly as they caressed the curves of her breasts.

"Ohhh." Samantha's breath caught as she tried to remain still.

"You're so soft," Shayne said so softly she barely heard him.

"And beautiful," Jackson smiled at her. "Look at these pretty little nipples."

When he touched a finger to one, Samantha almost jolted off the counter. Oh God. Her nipples had become so sensitive and needy that the least little touch sent an arrow of need straight to her pussy. She trembled and her stomach clenched almost painfully. Her panties had become even more soaked as her body prepared to be taken. When Shayne touched the other, she cried out at the exquisite pleasure.

Shayne jerked his hand away. "Did I hurt you?"

She saw the despair on his face. *This* was the crude animal that everyone talked about?

Nothing could have reassured her more. "No. You didn't hurt me. It felt too good." She took his big hand in hers and lifted it back to her breast, moaning as Jackson lightly pinched her other nipple. "Please touch me."

The heat in his eyes threatened to burn her. "You like when I touch you like this, baby?"

"Oh God. Yes."

They each touched her with one hand while removing her shirt and bra with the other. Soon she was bared to the waist and they both ran their hands over her, not missing an inch of exposed flesh.

"You have the prettiest breasts I've ever seen," Jackson told her softly. "I have to have a taste."

"I want to taste something else," Shayne's deep voice rumbled, making her shiver. "I want my mouth on your soft pussy." Oh God. The need in his voice sent her senses soaring as fresh moisture dampened her panties even more.

Her eyes popped open when he lifted her and with alarming ease, moved to the table and laid her on it before reaching for the fastening of her jeans.

Jackson leaned over her, pinching a nipple lightly. When she gasped and arched, he did it again. "You are so incredibly responsive. Your little nipples are just begging for my touch and you came before we even had you undressed. My brother and I are going to spend a lot of time getting to know your beautiful body, honey. And we're going to enjoy every minute of driving you wild."

Her jeans and panties slid down her legs and off until she lay naked on the kitchen table. She trembled even harder and her insides clenched. Jackson leaned down and took a nipple into his mouth, sucking it hard as his fingers closed over the other. Her hands tangled in his hair as she tried to hold him closer.

"Open your eyes."

Her eyes popped open at the steel in Shayne's tone. He'd never used that tone with her before. It caused a fresh rush of moisture to drip from her. Her pussy clenched uselessly and she thought she would die of need. How could they keep doing this to her?

The touch of his rough finger on her slit made her gasp. Those little sizzles started again and she knew another orgasm loomed close. She couldn't hold it off. So close.

"You're soaking wet," Shayne murmured huskily. He plunged a huge finger into her and she cried out as she came, her cries of release filling the room. He stroked the tender flesh, drawing out her release. She tightened on the finger inside her without meaning to. It stroked a spot inside her that sent her even higher. She couldn't escape the delicious feeling. Her body jolted, spasms of pure ecstasy racing through her.

The pleasure seemed to last forever and when it finally began to diminish, she opened her eyes, groaning to find them both staring at her. Jackson's face had tightened even more, but his eyes glittered with satisfaction as he continued to stroke her breasts.

Tremulously, she looked down to see Shayne's face had also tightened and looked even harsher than before. She closed her eyes, too embarrassed to face them. She probably seemed so gauche and inexperienced to them. They were probably used to women much more worldly and experienced, and she hadn't even been able to control herself, instead acting like some kind of sex starved virgin.

Mortified beyond belief, she lay there, not sure what to do. She still had Shayne's finger inside her, for God's sake! Trembling, she squeezed her eyes shut, unable to look at them after what had just happened.

"Open your eyes, Samantha. Look at me."

Samantha reluctantly opened her eyes, responding to the underlying steel in Shayne's voice. She felt his finger slide from her and watched, amazed, as he stuck it in his mouth and licked it clean.

He held her gaze for several long seconds before looking down at her mound. When his gaze met hers again, his eyes glittered fiercely, filled with need and emotion. "I could eat you alive."

Oh God! She started trembling all over again.

He lowered himself into the chair, effectively sitting between her spread legs. He bent, bringing his mouth closer and closer to her slit. When he finally reached his goal, he swiped it with his tongue, making her jolt and cry out. Oh God. It felt so incredible she could hardly stand it. He did it again and again, using his tongue to trace her folds repeatedly.

Jackson leaned over her, all trace of playfulness gone. "I can't wait to taste your sweet pussy, darlin'. I can't wait to make love to you." He tasted like sin, intoxicating her as his mouth moved over hers. His kisses and Shayne's touch made her forget everything but the pleasure and she could do nothing but hold on for the ride.

Shayne's tongue plunged inside her and she moaned, deep in her throat. Jackson swallowed her moan before lifting his head to watch her.

"You look so beautiful, Sam. All sweet and flushed. We're never letting you go. "

Shayne's hands slid under her bottom and lifted her to his mouth. "I could do this all day," he groaned. He began to devour her in earnest, erasing every rational thought from her mind. His tongue moved over her with alarming greed and she held on to Jackson in desperation.

Jackson leaned over her, nibbling at her jaw. "I want to feel your mouth on me, Sam. I want to feel that hot mouth take my cock inside. I want to feel that soft little tongue lick me."

Samantha's eyes opened to mere slits. "Oh! Yes." The erotic feel of Shayne using his mouth on her sensitive folds and clit, pressing his tongue inside her soaked pussy, robbed her of all reason. He held her in place, his large hands gentle but firm as he positioned her to his liking.

"Do you want Shayne to fuck that wet pussy?"

"Yesss."

The mouth on her slit paused and with one last swipe, Shayne stood to his full height over her. His face had tightened even more and his eyes appeared lit from within. He looked enormous standing over her, planted firmly between her naked thighs and she'd never felt so vulnerable. So feminine. So desired.

Her gaze slid to Jackson, too good looking to be real and watched as he fisted his cock in his hand, his eyes on hers as he slowly stroked. She lay there, unable to look away, mesmerized by the sight of his thick, hard cock moving closer. A glistening drop appeared at the tip, and she licked her lips, already anticipating the taste of him.

"Get those lips nice and wet for me, Sam." He moved closer and stroked her hair. "I can't wait to feel that mouth on my cock."

"Samantha."

She turned her head at Shayne's deep voice. "Do you really want this?"

Samantha moaned. "More than anything. Please. I can't stand it. Please, you have to do something."

Shayne's eyes burned even brighter. "We'll take care of you, baby. I promise I won't hurt you. Jackson will make sure."

She smiled at him even as she reached for Jackson's thick length. "I know you won't. But if you don't do something soon, I'm going to hurt *you*."

His look of surprise, followed by a quick grin stole her breath as Jackson reached for her, turning her face toward him.

"I can't wait, Sam. Please, honey. I need to take your mouth."

Suddenly ravenous for him, she opened her mouth wide to take him in, trembling with need as she felt Shayne move between her thighs. Hearing the sounds of his jeans being unzipped and foil ripping, she shook even harder.

Swiping her tongue over the head of Jackson's cock, she got her first taste of him. His groans of pleasure as she took him into her mouth made her hotter.

When she felt Shayne nudge at her entrance, she groaned. He began to press into her and muscles that hadn't been stretched for a long time began to burn.

"Easy, baby. I'll go real slow. Let me know if I'm hurting you." The unmistakable strain in his voice drove her even higher.

In answer, Samantha lifted her hips and drew Jackson even further into her mouth.

Shayne's big hands almost completely surrounded her as he gripped her hips again, lifting her to him. Jackson's hand moved to her breasts, caressing them and tugging at her nipples.

Shayne's shallow thrusts took him deeper, and she groaned at the incredible fullness. She tried to rock her hips to take even more of him, but he held her firmly.

"Easy, baby. I'll fill you."

Shayne's thrusts continued to press his thick length deeper and deeper. Moaning around Jackson's velvety hardness, she kept trying to tilt her hips to take him in faster. The unbelievable fullness had her entire body quivering.

The hands on her breasts continued to explore her, stroking and lightly pinching. Her moans, their deep groans and murmured encouragement filled the room.

"These breasts are so damned beautiful, Sam. Oh God, your mouth feels so good. Like hot velvet. Fuck. That tongue."

"Her pussy's so tight she's killing me," Shayne groaned, his voice barely recognizable. "So damned sweet. All these fucking little ripples. Jesus."

Samantha couldn't stay still. With her hands gripping Jackson's thighs for leverage, she squirmed on the table, so close, hanging on the edge of yet another orgasm.

"Fuck. I'm gonna come, Sam. If you don't want to swallow, you'd better let go. Now."

Samantha grabbed onto his thighs tighter. She needed all of him. Needed everything they could give her. The pull on her nipples intensified as Jackson groaned his completion. His cock pulsed and his erotic taste filled her mouth. She swallowed frantically, moaning as Shayne thrust further into her. Jackson's deep groans went on and on. "Never like this. Fuck. Oh God, Sam. So fucking good."

His groans and praise and the way he caressed her everywhere even afterward made her feel even more cared for. It also made her hotter. She squirmed harder, moaning in frustration and trying to take more of Shayne's thick steel inside her body. She needed all of him. She didn't want him to be careful. She wanted him to take her like he'd never taken another woman.

Shayne's big hands squeezed her bottom, halting her movement.

"No more, baby. I don't want to hurt you." Shayne sounded tortured as his thrusts increased in speed but he didn't go any deeper.

Jackson withdrew from her mouth and moved above her head, cupping her breasts and running his thumbs over her nipples. She cried out. "More, Shayne. Give me more."

The way his cock rubbed something inside her made her crazy. Her inner muscles burned from being stretched. Through eyes opened to slits, she could see his furious struggle for control. She didn't want him to feel he had to be careful with her.

She wanted him to need her so much, he forgot about control. She wanted to be able to take all of him.

She bucked on the table. "Shayne. More."

"Damn it, Samantha."

Jackson looked down at her. "Shayne, give her more."

"No, damn it."

Samantha cried out when he concentrated his thrusts on that sensitive spot inside her. "More, Shayne. Harder."

Between one thrust and the next, she went over again, crying out loudly as her body arched off the table. Every inch of her skin tingled with pleasure. Her inner muscles tightened on Shayne's cock, pleasuring her even more. It went on and on and she hoped it would never end. The tugs on her nipples added even more as did her lovers deep voices.

Samantha raised her hands over her head to grip the other side of the table as she dug her heels into Shayne's firm butt, forcing herself onto his thickness. She cried out at the delicious fullness.

With a bit off curse, he plunged into her and she screamed. He went so deep inside her, it seemed impossible. He cursed and attempted to withdraw from her. She dug her heels into him even harder, absently hearing their voices but couldn't focus on what they said. Her entire being had been taken over as one orgasm layered over another.

She shook, she cried out, she jolted in Jackson's arms as the incredible feeling burned through her. When Shayne's hands tightened and she heard his deep growl, she knew he'd followed, and burned even hotter as his cock pulsed inside her.

Shayne's hands dug into her hips, holding her tightly against him. His deep growl thrilled her and she knew he'd forgotten all about everything but his need for her.

Jackson's hands moved from her breasts to run over her still trembling body. She slowly came back down, completely sated, and struggled to catch her breath.

Except for big hands running over her, no one moved for several minutes. The sound of the refrigerator humming accompanied their harsh breathing. The sounds of the horses and the men outside finally got through to her and she grimaced, hoping that none of them had heard the sounds coming from the house.

Jackson brushed her damp hair back from her forehead, and smiled at her tenderly. "You're incredible, sweetheart. More than I ever hoped for. I can't wait to take you like Shayne just did. I'm so glad we found you," he murmured against her lips before taking them again in another of those long drugging kisses. By the time he lifted his head, her head spun again.

She smiled up at him. "I can't feel my fingers."

"Are you okay?" Shayne asked, looking at her worriedly.

Jackson chuckled. "She says she can't feel her fingers. I think we satisfied our little darlin'."

Samantha giggled as Shayne pulled her up from the table and into his arms, settling her on his lap, his softening length still deep inside her.

"I didn't hurt you?"

Samantha leaned back to look up at him. She put a hand to his cheek and smiled, wanting to erase his deep frown. "Of course not. I'm a grown woman, not a baby." She leaned forward and touched his lips with hers. "I can handle anything you can dish out, cowboy."

Shayne's lips twitched. "Don't kid yourself. You're just a tiny little thing." He blew out a breath and pulled her close. "What the hell am I going to do with you?"

Love me.

She had to bite back the words that threatened to escape as she snuggled into his embrace, smiling at Jackson as he stood watching them, a satisfied look on his face.

What had she done?

She'd just had sex with two men she'd fallen for but hadn't known very long, and felt more desired, more cared for than she ever had in her life. Shayne stood, withdrawing from her and holding her when she swayed. "Are you sure you're okay?"

Samantha nodded, trying hard not to show her disappointment that Shayne seemed like he couldn't wait to turn her over to Jackson. He righted his clothes and when he looked at her again, his face had once again become cold and remote. "Are you sure you're okay? I didn't hurt you?"

Samantha moved away and reached for her clothes. Shayne's cool attitude stung. His demeanor had changed completely again. A few minutes earlier she would have sworn that he cared for her. Apparently, she'd been mistaken.

"I'm fine."

She winced inwardly when Shayne nodded abruptly and strode from the room.

Jackson's lips moved to her neck. "We have a few things to do to get ready for Saturday. Once we pay these guys off, we won't have to worry about your safety anymore."

She nodded, trying not to show her hurt. But Jackson saw it.

He lifted her chin, kissing her lightly. "Shayne cares for you, honey. We both do, but he just has a harder time showing it." He smiled and rubbed her shoulder. "You'll see. Everything will work out. We just have to get rid of these men who threatened to hurt you. And once Shayne realizes how you feel about him and that he *is* gentle with you, everything will be fine. I promise."

Samantha nodded. "I'm sure you're right." She forced herself to smile at him before he turned and walked out.

As soon as he left, her smile fell. She wasn't sure of anything except that when she left here, her heart would be in tatters.

* * * *

The men came in just as she'd finished setting the table. Moving to the sink, she carefully kept her back to the room as they passed through on the way to take their showers. She'd been nervous all day about sitting at the dinner table with them, not knowing what to expect. Still unsettled over her earlier reaction, she didn't feel ready to face them.

Jackson came back into the kitchen first, his damp hair combed back. He and Shayne always dressed in jeans and t-shirts after their showers and both always took her breath away. Before she knew what he'd planned, he turned her and wrapped his arms around her, pulling her close. She stiffened involuntarily. When he did nothing more than hold her, she gradually relaxed in his embrace.

When he started running his hands over her back, she melted into him. It felt so good to have him hold her this way, and she just couldn't fight it.

Her nipples poked at his chest and although she knew he had to feel it, he didn't acknowledge it. He leaned back and with a finger under her chin, tilted her face to his. "Hi, honey."

His mouth covered hers, and she leaned into him. He held her head tilted as he explored her mouth, swallowing her moan and pulling her more tightly against him. When he finally lifted his head, she blinked, dazed. God, he could kiss.

He smiled at her wickedly and bit her lip, tweaking a throbbing nipple and making her gasp, before moving away. With a pat on her bottom, he moved to sit at the table and started to fill his plate, looking from her to Shayne.

Shayne had already taken his seat and she looked over to find him staring at her. "Come here, Samantha."

Already throbbing with need, she knew she'd be no match for him. Thinking about the incredible lovemaking and then his cool attitude afterward, she began to tremble. "W-why?"

Shayne's face hardened. "Forget it." He turned his chair to the table and started filling his plate.

Too unsure of herself and his feelings, she didn't feel up to dealing with him right now. "I'm not hungry. I'm going to my room."

"Sit down, Sam." Jackson's voice lashed out like a whip.

Samantha froze. "I want to go to my room." She bolted for the door.

Shayne moved fast for such a big man. He shot out his arm, catching her around the waist and pulled her onto his lap.

She struggled briefly, but of course she couldn't budge. Moisture dripped from her as she sat on his rock hard thighs. The heat of his body ignited hers. But she couldn't forget how he'd been with her after their lovemaking earlier.

"What do you want from me?"

Jackson leaned forward. "We want to talk about this afternoon."

"I don't want to talk about it." Especially, since she hadn't figured it out herself.

She trembled as Shayne ran a rough finger softly over her arm.

"If you're afraid of me, I won't ever touch you again."

"I'm not afraid of you," she said softly.

He rubbed a hand down her arm, asking tenderly, "Aren't you going to eat your dinner?"

"I'm not hungry."

"You're shaking. You don't have to be afraid of me."

Samantha felt her face burn and ducked her head. "I'm not."

"Sam, look at me," Jackson ordered softly.

When Samantha looked up, her insides clenched at the need on his face.

"Shayne and I both care for you very much. You know that, don't you?"

Samantha shook her head. "I can't do this. We hardly know each other."

Jackson frowned. "Yes, we do. We've learned enough about each other living together. We'll learn more."

He smiled at her so tenderly. "Come here, honey."

When Shayne let her go, she stood and moved toward Jackson. "Please say what you have to say so I can go to my room. I have some things to do." She just had to get away from them and think.

Jackson pulled her onto his lap and cradled her against his chest. "I love you. I've never said that to another woman before. I want you to stay here with us. Be our woman." He lowered his mouth to hers. Held tightly against his chest, she opened up to him as he took her mouth hungrily.

She simply melted. Clinging to him, she gave him everything. The muscles under her hand shifted as he pulled her even closer. By the time he lifted his head, her body hummed. When a hand covered her breast and began stroking, she moaned helplessly.

He unbuttoned her shirt and quickly undid her bra, baring her. "I want you so badly. I've never wanted anything more."

The emotions that played across his handsome face heated her blood even more.

"Oh, Jackson. I'm afraid I love you, too." She smiled tearfully at him. "I tried not to. It's too soon. How can we love each other?" She frowned up at him. "Maybe it's just sex."

Jackson smiled at her so tenderly, it brought tears to her eyes. "I've had sex before, Sam. Many times. Trust me, it's not just sex for me." He cupped her breast, stroking his thumb lightly over her nipple, smiling indulgently when she gasped. "And I don't think you're the kind of woman who could respond the way you do to someone unless you love them."

Samantha looked over to see Shayne watching them silently, his eyes glittering. Trying not to be disappointed, she looked back up at Jackson to see him frowning at his brother. He must have felt her gaze, back down at her.

His smile looked forced. "Everything will work out. Eat. Before I give into temptation and have *you* for dinner."

Chapter Five

On Saturday morning the tension in the air could be cut with a knife. Samantha kept glancing back and forth between Shayne and Jackson, waiting for one of them to say something.

When both remained silent, she finally blurted, "I heard what happened last night."

Both men stopped eating, glancing at each other before looking at her.

Jackson frowned when Shayne rose to get more coffee, leaving him to answer. "I thought you were asleep. Don't worry about Pete. He didn't get off the ranch."

Samantha stared down at her plate, pushing her eggs around. "He was drunk, wasn't he? I heard what he said."

When both men cursed, she looked up. "He didn't say anything that everyone else isn't thinking."

She'd woken to the sounds of a scuffle and harsh words. Petey had gotten drunk and wanted to go to town to get laid. She hadn't recognized the voices of the men Petey had argued with, but heard enough to know they'd stopped him from sneaking off the ranch.

A few minutes later, she'd heard Jackson's voice and Shayne's deeper tone ordering her brother back to the bunkhouse.

Petey had gotten even angrier. "Easy for you guys to say. You get laid. You're both fucking my sister."

Samantha had already started for the door, intending to go outside to try to reason with him. Hearing his words, she froze, mortified and hurt beyond belief.

The following silence had been deafening, followed by a thud and the sound of a body falling.

Shayne's icy, "Put him to bed," had sent a shiver through her and she'd moved like an old woman back to bed.

It had taken hours to fall back to sleep. She'd gotten up early, still upset and nervous about the meeting tonight.

It hadn't surprised her that both Jackson and Shayne had come downstairs only minutes behind her.

She dropped her fork and picked up her coffee to warm her icy hands. Nothing could have surprised her more than the touch of Shayne's hands on her shoulders. Trembling, she put down her cup, afraid she would spill it. Her eyes closed of their own volition when she felt his warm breath on her neck.

"There isn't a man on the place who doesn't know how Jackson and I feel about you."

He bent and dropped a hard kiss on her lips before straightening and moving back to his seat. He sat, calmly sipping his coffee, raising a brow at her continued silence.

Ruffled, she opened and closed her mouth several times, but didn't know what to say. Finally, she managed an, "Oh."

Her face burned when she realized how stupid she'd sounded.

Shayne surprised the hell out of her again by throwing his head back and laughing. A glance at Jackson told her he was just as amazed.

Her heart melted. When Shayne stopped laughing and began to look a little self conscious, she crossed her arms over her chest and stuck her tongue out at him, playfully. "Stinker."

His eyes flared, all signs of self consciousness gone. "Be careful waving that tongue around, Samantha. You could find yourself in big trouble."

Samantha batted her eyes. "Are you flirting with me?"

Both men laughed and the tension disappeared.

* * * *

Samantha prepared thick sandwiches for lunch. Throughout the meal, Jackson flirted outrageously and even Shayne teased her. She suspected they did it to ease her fears about the coming evening and because of what she'd overheard the night before. Although she appreciated the effort and teased them back, nothing could get rid of the apprehension that churned her stomach.

"Come here, Sam."

Samantha looked up at Jackson, dropping the sandwich she'd been steadily breaking into little pieces.

He pulled her onto his lap and lifted his own sandwich to her lips. "Open."

She smiled and took a bite, leaning against him as she chewed. He and Shayne finished their sandwiches and each started on another.

Between bites, Jackson unbuttoned her shirt, stroking each inch of skin he revealed. By the time he finally pulled the two sides apart and unclasped her bra, she'd become a mass of need.

"I love these pretty breasts," Jackson drawled, stroking a nipple.

Lying across Jackson's lap, his arm supporting her back, Samantha lost herself in sensation as his hands continued to roam.

She couldn't keep from moaning when his hand slid between her legs. "I want you so damned much. As soon as we get back from paying these guys off, I'm taking you to bed. I can't wait to get inside this hot little pussy."

"Oh, Jackson. I want you, too."

"You'd better be ready when I get back because as soon as I walk through that door, you're mine."

She laughed as Jackson helped her up, slapping her bottom teasingly. He made her feel so good. When she started to move away, he gripped her hips and pulled her back against him. She froze when he ran one hand over her bottom while holding her in place with the other.

"I love your ass, Sam. Has anyone ever taken you there?"

"N-no." She shuddered when his hand moved down her jean clad bottom and pressed between her legs. Moaning, she grabbed onto the table when he began to press against her forbidden opening."

"Do you know how good it's gonna feel when Shayne and I take you together? One of us will be fucking your pussy while the other is fucking your tight ass."

"Oh God." When Jackson reached around to cover her breasts, she gripped his forearm as her legs started to tremble.

"I'm tasting, and then I'm taking that sweet pussy as soon as we get home. Shayne and I are going to start working on that ass. Aren't we, Shayne?"

Samantha looked over to see Shayne watching his brother's hands tug at her nipples. He looked up and met her gaze before letting his glittering eyes move over her. When he looked back up at her, his eyes blazed. "Yes."

Kissing the top of her head, Jackson released her. When she started righting her clothing, Shayne spoke.

"No. Come here. It's my turn."

When she moved close, he pulled her onto his lap, and held her as Jackson had. He manipulated her nipples, alternately stroking, pinching and tugging as though gauging her response to each sensation.

She thought she would die from the pleasure.

His big hands moved over her gently, but firmly, touching every inch of bare skin.

"Shayne, please. I can't stand it anymore."

He unfastened her jeans and lifted her enough to push them to her knees.

Samantha felt his fingers brush over her mound and tried to part her thighs, but the jeans around her knees prevented it. Whimpering with frustration, she struggled to kick them off.

Shayne pulled them the rest of the way off and gripped her hip, flipping her to her stomach.

Samantha froze. "What are you doing?"

"I've been dying to have a good look at this ass."

His words and tone had her literally dripping. She moaned, readily parting her thighs as Shayne's callused hand moved over her bottom. He stroked her over and over, not missing a single spot, making her entire bottom tingle. She couldn't lie still, squirming on his lap as she tried to find relief. "Please, Shayne."

She heard the scrape of a chair as Jackson stood. She watched his legs as he moved around the table. When she could no longer see him, she felt his hands on her thighs, parting them even more and moving between them.

Her moans and whimpers filled the room as she kicked her legs, desperate to come. "Damn it. Stop teasing me."

Jackson chuckled. "Wild little thing, isn't she?"

"Spread her."

"Oh God." Her clit throbbed even more as fresh moisture flowed from her.

Samantha gasped as Jackson's hands moved to cover the cheeks of her bottom and spread them, revealing her most private place.

"What are you going to do?" Her voice came out breathlessly as she tried to move, but Shayne held her in place.

"Easy, Samantha. I just want to explore your bottom a little. I won't hurt you."

He'd spoken in that dark, erotic tone making her slit even wetter. Almost mindless with the need to come, she shuddered, teetering on the edge as a thick finger slid into her pussy. Once coated with her juices, it withdrew, only to slide up and press against her puckered opening.

"Jesus," Jackson breathed. "Sam, your ass is beautiful."

A chill went through her as Shayne exerted pressure and pressed the tip of his finger past the tight ring of muscle.

"Ohhh. Ahhh. Oh my God." Samantha groaned, kicking her feet as he continued his slow press into her.

"Jesus, she's tight," Shayne growled.

Samantha couldn't keep up with the sensations bombarding her. Little tingles of pleasure accompanied the burn radiating from her anus. She trembled uncontrollably, chills racing through her even as a fire raged inside.

She trembled harder with each millimeter of Shayne's finger that pressed into her.

It felt so naughty, so erotic, being exposed this way, being opened, her anus invaded. She felt so vulnerable and yet so incredibly desired.

Jackson stroked her bottom cheeks. "Easy, honey. A little more. Hell, I'm about to come in my jeans just watching."

Samantha's toes curled as Shayne worked the rest of his finger into her.

"I thought about doing this the first time I saw you." Shayne's voice sounded harsh. "Your ass is perfect. Firm and soft."

Samantha groaned, gripping his leg even harder when he began stroking her anus with slow deliberation. Jackson slid a hand between her legs and pressed a finger inside her pussy. She cried out at the unfamiliar fullness.

"Can you imagine spanking this ass the next time Sam's a bad girl?" Jackson asked as he began to stroke her pussy.

Shayne's strokes got faster. "And then fucking it."

Samantha kicked her feet, feeling her orgasm approach. Wild with need, she cried out repeatedly as their stroking continued. When a finger slid over her soaked clit and began stroking, she screamed hoarsely as she went over.

Tightening on both of them, she bucked on Shayne's lap as wave after wave of intense pleasure washed over her. The burn and fullness in her bottom added to her pleasure, creating a sensation she'd never experienced.

Finally spent, she lay over Shayne's lap, breathing heavily. He and Jackson both withdrew from her, eliciting a weak groan. She tried to get up, assuming they would be anxious to have sex, but Shayne's firm hand kept her in place.

"Stay still, Samantha." He continued to caress her back and bottom for several minutes before lifting her to stand beside him. He bent forward to tug a nipple between his lips before standing. "Don't worry about dinner for us. We're going to eat in town. As soon as we pay off these guys, we'll be back."

Jackson moved behind her to cup her breasts, dropping a kiss on her shoulder. "You're in big trouble tonight, baby."

* * * *

Freshly bathed and moisturized, Samantha donned her robe and studied her reflection in the mirror. Her skin had become flushed and her eyes sparkled with excitement.

She loved Jackson and couldn't wait for him to make love to her tonight. He'd made his intentions and his feelings perfectly clear and she was filled with excitement to start their lives together.

She didn't know what she would do about Shayne. She loved him just as much, but her love for him didn't sit as comfortably as it did with Jackson, if what she felt for Jackson could really be considered comfortable. She knew Shayne cared for her but didn't know if he would ever be willing to let go and give her his all.

And she couldn't live with anything less. She couldn't maintain a relationship with someone who held parts of himself back from her and always felt he had to be careful around her. He desired her, she knew, but that wouldn't be enough for her.

Pulling the lapels of the robe tightly closed, she started to pace her bedroom. How would she be able to go on living here with Jackson if she and Shayne didn't get things sorted out between them? She wouldn't be an occasional lay for him while committing herself to his brother. Still working on dealing with the fact that she may find herself involved in a relationship with two men, she knew there were some things she just couldn't accept.

Shayne wanting to fuck her while remaining aloof was one of them.

She needed to calm down and think. Walking into the living room with the intention of finding a movie on television, she heard a slight sound.

Before she could react, she found herself grabbed forcefully from behind. A hand over her mouth muffled her scream as she fought like a wild woman to be free. The steel band around her waist pressed hard on her ribs.

"So we meet again."

The deep voice boomed next to her ear as the thick arm around her waist tightened. Oh God! It was Bruce Graham.

Big and heavily muscled, he held her easily. She couldn't even turn to look at him. Realizing that all her struggles managed to do was part her robe, she froze, stiff with terror.

He caressed her waist, his hand moving threateningly higher toward her breasts. "If you scream, I'll hurt you. Do you understand?"

Fighting nausea, Samantha struggled to breathe. She nodded, her terror growing. If only Shayne and Jackson would get home!

When he lifted his hand slowly from her mouth, she licked her dry lips, tasted blood and had to swallow before speaking. "What do you want? I gave Shayne your message."

The hand he'd removed from her mouth covered her breast. Her breath caught as he squeezed, bruising her, and she shuddered in revulsion.

"I thought you would like that," he chuckled. "A woman who takes two men to her bed wants it bad. Not so high and mighty now, are you? When we get away from here, I'll show you what it feels like to have a real man fuck you. You don't need two to please you when you've got one as good as me."

Samantha bit her lip to silence the whimpers that rasped her throat as he continued to knead her breast. "What do you want?"

"I want *you*." He leaned down and bit her shoulder, making her cry out, her mind almost numb with horror.

This can't be happening to me.

"I see you like that, too. We'll have to have some fun while I convince your men to sign the contract."

Calm down, Sam. Think!

"Why are you doing this?"

With a muscled arm around her waist and another on her chest, palming her breast, he forced her across the room, easily overcoming her struggles. "I need the commission from the oil well your men are going to let my company dig. Don't worry. They'll get rich. But, I get a nice cut when they sign. Shayne doesn't want to listen to me. He will when he finds out I have his woman."

Samantha's struggles intensified as they got closer to the door. She couldn't let him take her out of here. She'd be dead for sure. "They won't sign. I'm just the housekeeper. Just go. They'll be home any minute."

"Stop struggling, damn you. You're coming with me. Don't make me hurt you. You're more than the housekeeper. I saw the way Jackson touched you in the grocery store. I heard what he told those women."

"No. I'm not going with you." Samantha fought with everything she had. Grabbing a lamp on the end table by the door, she struck out wildly, surprised when she managed to hit him hard enough that he loosened his grip. She fought even harder, hearing him curse as he couldn't hold onto her, his hands sliding off her satin robe.

Screaming at the top of her lungs, she scrambled for freedom. She didn't take two steps before he tackled her from behind, the weight of his body knocking the air out of her lungs.

Oh God! Please let one of the ranch hands have heard my screams.

"After I fuck you, and they sign the contract, I'm going to kill you, you little bitch! As soon as I get you out of here, I'm going to fuck you so hard, you won't think of giving me any more of this shit."

Trapped on her stomach, Samantha struggled to catch her breath while she fought him. He held her down while reaching down for her robe and lifting it to expose her naked bottom.

"You have a beautiful ass, bitch. Do you let your men fuck you there?"

When his thighs separated hers and his hand moved between them, Samantha screamed, tears blurring her vision as she kicked out wildly.

"No! Oh God. No! Let go of me."

She saw a very large pair of cowboy boots, heard a loud roar and suddenly she was free. Scrambling to her knees, she struggled to get away, fighting off the hands that tried to grab her. Screaming, with tears blurring her vision, she fought like a woman possessed. She couldn't let him touch her again!

"Sam, it's me, honey. Oh, baby. It's me. It's Jackson, Sam. I've got you."

* * * *

Jackson barely glanced at Shayne as he fought the other man and concentrated solely on calming Samantha. He could tell when his voice finally got through to her. She slumped in his arms, crying brokenly and gripping his shirt frantically.

He pulled her close, watching over her shoulder as Shayne literally picked the other man up and threw him against the wall. Although the other man was big, he didn't stand a chance against Shayne. His brother towered over the intruder, the rage and power behind his punches not even giving the other man a chance to fight back. Within a minute, the other man lay unconscious with a still enraged Shayne standing over him.

Jackson paid them little attention, focusing all his attention on the trembling woman in his arms. He'd never been so scared in his entire life as when he and Shayne pulled up and heard her screams. He buried his face in her hair, rubbing his hands up and down her back, trying his best to soothe her.

She'd already become the most important thing in his life. And it had happened so quickly he hadn't gotten used to it yet. This made him realize just how much he'd come to love her already. It scared him to death. He didn't know what he would have done if anything had happened to her.

Realizing that he shook almost as hard as she did, he forced himself to calm down. His woman needed him and he would be there for her. He knew he would fall apart later. The scene he and Shayne had walked in on would give him nightmares for weeks to come.

Pete spoke from behind him, startling Samantha. Jackson crooned to her again, still stroking her and making sure her face stayed hidden against him. He didn't want her to see the unconscious man in the living room. He watched Shayne's struggle for control, having no doubt about his brother's ability to rein it in.

Pete touched Samantha's shoulder comfortingly, his eyes haunted. "I'll call the sheriff. I found Doug outside. He was knocked out."

Jackson nodded, watching his brother. The incredible rage on his face kept even the seasoned ranch hands from approaching him. He'd never in his life seen his brother like this.

Shayne's eyes darted wildly as though looking for something else to hit, his rage barely spent. His fists at his sides trembled as he moved forward, his face a mask of agony as he reached for Samantha. At the last second, he stopped short, looking at Jackson with eyes full of both pain and fury. Looking down at his still trembling hands, he said softly, as though in a daze, "I can't touch her. I'll hurt her. I can't...I'll wait for the sheriff out front."

Jackson called after him but Shayne ignored him and continued out the door. They couldn't go on this way. Jackson knew Shayne loved Samantha almost more than he could stand. He wouldn't be able to hide it from her much longer.

His brother needed him now but Samantha needed him more. He didn't want her to look up and see the unconscious man, so he carried her from the room and into his bedroom, jerking the blanket off of the bed to wrap around her.

Her whimpers tore at him. He spoke softly to her, pulling her tightly against him as she continued to shake. "It's all over, sweetheart. Nobody can hurt you now."

When she looked up at him with tear filled eyes, his heart broke. "Are you hurt anywhere? Let me see you, honey." He watched helplessly as she struggled to gather herself.

"No. I'm okay. I'm okay. I was so scared. I couldn't fight him. He was so strong. Please just hold me a little bit longer."

Jackson tightened his arms around her. "I'll hold you as long as you want."

"Where's Shayne?" She pushed against his chest to look up at him. "He's not hurt, is he?"

Jackson pulled her back against him. "No. He's not hurt, at least on the outside." He took a deep breath, letting it out slowly. "He beat the hell out of the guy who attacked you, Sam. He's still so mad he's shaking. He went outside. He's afraid he'll hurt you."

"He won't."

The absolute conviction in her voice relieved him as nothing else could have. "He and I both love you so much, Samantha. But we can never be happy and settle down until Shayne believes that."

Samantha looked up at him through her lashes. "He needs me. I need to go to him."

Jackson hugged her to him, loving the feel of her soft, warm and *safe* in his arms. "I don't know how we got lucky enough to have you but I can't imagine my life without you in it anymore." He brushed her hair back from her face, frowning when he saw her cheek.

"You're hurt. Your cheek is all red and swollen. Lie down so I can get you some ice."

Samantha shook her head and pushed off of his lap. "I need to go to Shayne."

"Later. Let me—"

"No. I want to go to him now while he's still mad. I need to show him that I'm not afraid of him."

Jackson sighed. He knew it was probably the best thing for both of them but he wanted to take care of her cheek, and he hated the idea that she would walk past the man who'd attacked her.

"Let me get some ice for your cheek and I'll walk you out."

"Okay. Hurry. I don't want Shayne sitting out there by himself."

Jackson got her the ice and kept her face against his chest as they crossed the living room. He heard the sheriff pull up as they got to the door. He reluctantly released her. "Go to Shayne, honey."

She turned to him. "Aren't you coming?"

Jackson shook his head. "I'm going to talk to the sheriff to give you and Shayne a few minutes alone. He needs you, Sam."

When Samantha nodded and turned toward Shayne, Jackson hoped his brother and their woman would find a way to help each other.

* * * *

Shayne heard the front door open and looked over, groaning when he saw Samantha. "Go back inside," he growled. He hadn't yet calmed down enough to trust himself around her. And where in the hell was Jackson going? Why wasn't he taking care of her?

Wrapped in a blanket, her feet bare, and a towel held to her face, Samantha looked so small and defenseless. The rage inside him started to build again when he thought about what he'd walked in on. That someone would *dare* to touch her filled him with a fury like he'd never felt before.

"Go to Jackson," he all but snarled at her.

She stopped as though hitting a brick wall.

His knees actually buckled at the hurt in her eyes. The well of tears broke his heart.

"Oh. I understand." She turned and started to walk away.

The tremor in her voice threatened to bring him to his knees. "What do you understand?"

She paused and looked over her shoulder, not meeting his eyes. "He touched me and so now you don't want to."

The pain in her voice nearly undid him. "What? Are you crazy?"

Before he knew it, he'd covered the distance between them and lifted her high into his arms. He winced when she cried out.

Way to go, Shayne. Grab at a woman who's just been attacked.

He looked toward Jackson for help but his brother had his back to him, talking to the sheriff. He looked back down at the bundle in his arms. "I'm sorry, baby. I didn't mean to scare you. I'm not any good at this stuff. You should have stayed with Jackson."

Samantha looked up at him tearfully. "I understand. Just put me down and I'll go back inside."

Damn it.

He would rather cut off his own arm than have her look at him that way. "Samantha, baby. Please don't cry. I don't know what to do for you."

"I just want you to hold me, but I understand if you don't want to."

"Damn it, Samantha. I want to hold you more than anything but I'm afraid I'll hurt you. Did you see what happened in there? I knocked a man out with my bare hands just by picking him up and throwing him against a wall. I couldn't stand it if I hurt you. I'm too rough."

When her little hand came out and caressed his cheek, he felt as though he'd been given the most precious gift in the world. He could literally feel the anger drain away.

"You saved me. And the only way you could hurt me is by not wanting me anymore."

His heart melted as his insides clenched in fear. Samantha needed him and he didn't know what to do for her. Carrying her to the swing, he sat, wrapping the blanket securely around her. He took the ice filled towel from her and gently held it to her cheek. "Does it hurt a lot, baby?"

"No. I think I might have hit it on the floor when he tackled me. It doesn't really hurt though."

"I saw his hand between your legs. Did he hurt you there?"

She paled, trembling. "I'm okay. You stopped him before he could…you know."

She looked up at him so trustingly, as though she knew he would take care of everything. The trust in her eyes as she looked at him made him feel ten feet tall. With a sense of relief, he saw Jackson and the sheriff headed toward him. *This* he could handle.

He lifted Samantha slightly with every intention of handing her off to his brother, when she shuddered and laid a hand on his chest, dropping her head onto his shoulder and hiding her face in his neck.

She'd wrapped herself around his heart so fast that he'd had no defense against her. He could see that he would spend the rest of his life wrapped just as tightly around her little finger.

"Is she hurt? We should get her to the hospital for them to check her out, along with Doug."

The sheriff's booming voice made Samantha flinch and Shayne instinctively tightened his arms around her.

She hid her face in his neck, gripping his shirt. "No. I don't want to go anywhere. Please don't make me."

He adjusted the towel and the blanket, pulling her close. "I won't, baby. You can stay right here."

Ignoring the sheriff's look of surprise, he put the swing in motion, holding Samantha tightly against him, as the sheriff and his deputies went into the house.

* * * *

Jackson watched as the sheriff questioned Shayne and Samantha. He'd already been questioned and except for adding a comment here and there, remained silent. Shayne still held Samantha on his lap, cradling her against him as he would a newborn.

He rocked her the entire time the sheriff questioned them, adjusting the blanket around her and holding the ice to her cheek.

Going through the chain of events, they told their story, pausing only when they got to the part where the man had touched Samantha.

"I have to know what happened," the sheriff told her. "I need the whole story. You have to tell me what you saw and heard."

Shayne's features tightened dangerously. "Don't talk to her that way. Ever. If she doesn't want to talk about it, then we don't talk about it."

"No, Shayne. He's right."

Samantha sat up, holding the blanket around her. Shayne's anger had died down and she didn't want him getting mad again. She'd stayed on his lap, loving the way he held her and cuddled her close to him, knowing he needed to see the gentleness in himself that everyone else saw.

"The man tackled me from behind and had me on the floor, face down and, and…" She took a deep breath. This would be harder than she'd thought.

"He pulled my robe up and pushed his hand between my legs. Shayne got him off of me. He told me he was going to kidnap me until they signed the contract."

They'd already explained about the oil company and the man confronting her in the store and in the parking lot. Evidently, Shayne had been telling him no for months.

"He was going to hold me until Shayne and Jackson signed to let his company drill here. He was going to rape me and after they signed, he was going to kill me."

When her voice broke, Jackson moved to sit beside Shayne on the swing and pulled her feet on his lap, stroking her leg. Shayne pulled her even closer. She didn't know if she could have handled this without them. Their touch comforted more than anything else could have. If they hadn't gotten there when they did...

But they did.

She had to remember that and not dwell on something that could have happened.

They took Bruce Graham away. Shayne hid her face in his neck as they escorted the handcuffed man out. The whole thing seemed like a bad dream and she just wanted to block it out of her mind.

When everyone left, they went back into the house to find that Petey and a few of the ranch hands had cleaned up the mess. The other ranch hands had gone back out, but Petey stayed behind.

Samantha went into the kitchen, feeling more comfortable there, and sank into a chair.

Petey knelt next to her and gripped her hand. "Sam, I'm so sorry."

Samantha blinked. She'd never heard her brother apologize about anything. "It's okay, Petey. It's not your fault."

She saw him look over her shoulder to where she knew Shayne and Jackson stood. "Yes, damn it. It is my fault. All of this is my fault. Borrowing money from those guys. Gambling. Putting you in danger." His eyes looked tortured. "I know you heard what I said about you and Shayne and Jackson. I'm sorry. I didn't mean it."

Samantha had never seen her brother this way, and knew it had a lot to do with the men standing behind her. "It's okay, Petey. Everything worked out."

"Yeah, but not because of me. I promise you, Sam, I'm going to be different from now on." He glanced over her shoulder again. "I'm not going to get into any more trouble. It's time for me to grow up and stop depending on you to take care of me."

Samantha smiled and leaned down to kiss his cheek, for the first time noticing the bruising there. She touched it lightly. "What happened?"

Petey turned red. "Shayne cleaned my clock for what I said about you. I deserved it." He stood and kissed the top of her head. "I'd better get back to work. I'll be around to check on you later."

Samantha nodded, watching as he started out.

Halfway out the door, Petey turned back. "Oh, Sam. I need one more favor." She felt the men shift behind her as Petey grinned. "Can you start calling me 'Pete'?"

After he left, she stood. "I need another shower."

After showering, she got dressed and went back out to the kitchen, unsurprised to find both Shayne and Jackson waiting for her.

Shayne handed her a glass of milk and seated her at the kitchen table, dropping into the seat next to her. He never said a word, just sat next to her silently, running his fingers over her arm.

Jackson touched her shoulder and sat on her other side. "Would you like to talk?"

"No." They'd already been over it with the sheriff and each other and she didn't want to talk about it anymore.

So, Shayne and Jackson took her out with them when they went to check on the horses and they went for a walk, talking to her about the cattle and horses and answering her questions.

They told her that the men who Petey had borrowed money from were now in jail.

She needed to talk about anything but what happened earlier. "I've been meaning to ask you something. Why is this called the Dakota Ranch? Your last name isn't Dakota."

Jackson's arm tightened around her. "My grandfather started this ranch. He named it after my grandmother. Her name was Dakota."

"He must have loved her very much to name the ranch after her."

Jackson turned her to face him, pulling her close. "He did. I know what he felt like. I love you, Sam. I want to spend the rest of my life with you."

"Oh, Jackson."

The look in his eyes told her everything she needed to know and warmed her from within. His mouth took hers, gently at first as though not wanting to scare her and then more forcefully. Her breasts swelled and her nipples tightened against his chest, begging for attention.

After what had happened earlier, she needed this. Needed to feel his hands on her. She needed to be touched with desire. With heat. With love.

Chapter Six

Jackson lifted her in his arms and started toward the house. Samantha couldn't help but look over his shoulder for Shayne. Her smile fell when she saw him walking back toward the stable.

Once inside, Jackson strode straight to his bedroom. He laid her gently on the bed and slowly began to undress her. His mouth touched every inch he uncovered, nipping and nibbling his way around her body, making erotic promises and heating her blood. He moved slowly, loving her gently as though afraid of startling her. Every touch of his mouth on her erased more and more of the ugliness she'd endured earlier.

He pushed the hair back from her forehead and touched his lips lightly to her sore cheek.

He stared down at her tenderly for several long seconds before gently flipping her to her stomach. At her automatic protest, he crooned next to her ear. "It's me, honey. I want to make you feel good. I love you. Just feel, Sam. There's nobody here but you and me. Close your eyes."

Samantha closed her eyes and felt Jackson's lips move down her back. Her desire had waned when he flipped her over, reminding her too much of what had happened earlier.

But as his lips moved over her back, his hands came around her and she arched so he could touch her breasts. His callused palms felt incredible against her nipples. He murmured to her as he stroked, nibbling and licking at her back and shoulders.

"You are so soft. These breasts are so soft and smooth. I love these hard little nipples," he growled in her ear as he lightly pinched them.

Samantha groaned, her hands fisting on the bedclothes. When he moved down her body, she felt his lips on her bottom and tightened involuntarily.

"Easy, Sam. Say my name. Who's making love to you?"

"Jackson. What are you doing? Oh God!"

His mouth moved lower, as did his hands as he separated the cheeks of her bottom and slid his tongue between them.

"Jackson," she moaned. "Oh, what are you doing to me?"

"Lovin' you, darlin'. Just lovin' you. I want you to think of just me touching you here. The rest doesn't exist."

Samantha groaned. She'd never felt such a thing before. He spread her thighs wider and settled between them. When his tongue touched her puckered opening, she squealed and would have jerked away if he hadn't been holding her.

"Jackson, ohhhh!"

"Do you know how good it's going to feel when I take you here?"

Samantha tensed. "Jackson, I—"

"Not yet, honey. Relax and let me make you feel good."

Samantha had no choice. Jackson held her in place as his mouth moved over her, sliding down and lifting her so he could lick her folds.

On her knees now, with her legs spread wide, she now lay completely open to Jackson's ministrations. Her moans sounded loud in the room as he used his mouth on her ruthlessly now, giving her no choice but to think of nothing but him and what he did to her.

Her first orgasm hit her, surprising her with its speed. Jackson pressed his tongue inside her and she could feel her inner muscles ripple around it.

Her cries filled the room as she shuddered. Oh God. It felt so good. She felt Jackson move and heard the sound of his belt hitting the floor. "Jackson. Hurry."

He moved away briefly, and she heard the rip of foil. Seconds later, he was back.

She arched into him and felt his hand slide between her thighs, spreading her moisture. When a thick finger pressed against her forbidden opening at the same time another touched her clit, Samantha's senses soared. As soon as thoughts of what happened earlier started to seep in, a devastating stroke of her clit and the sound of his voice pushed them away.

"You're so wet, darlin.' This tight little hole wants to open for me, doesn't it, honey?"

"Oh God. Yessss. Jackson. Take me."

She groaned as Jackson began to press into both openings at the same time, his thick cock in her pussy, his demonic finger in her bottom. She thought of nothing but what he did to her. Thought of no one but him. He spoke to her the entire time, his deep voice demanding she say his name over and over.

Her pussy clenched on him, trying to pull him in faster, but he wouldn't be rushed. His slow smooth strokes had her crying out for more. She felt taken as never before, everything opening to him so completely and she couldn't prevent it. Didn't want to. She just wanted more.

"Your ass is so tight," Jackson groaned hoarsely. "Your pussy is so tight, so hot. Christ, I could stay inside you forever."

His words poured over her like warm honey. The fire inside her burned out of control and when his thrusts deepened, she could do nothing but feel. All thoughts of what had happened earlier dimmed, being replaced by the love and desire Jackson forced her to focus on.

His thick cock stretched her inner walls deliciously. When he found the secret place inside her that drove her wild, her cries intensified. Oh God. How did he do this to her?

Her anus burned at his steady strokes, the sensation adding to the chaos raging inside her. Grabbing handfuls of the bedcovers, she pushed back, a hoarse scream of pleasure erupting at the incredible fullness.

"That's it, honey. Take me. Fuck, you're so incredible."

When he reached under her again to stroke her folds, her body trembled helplessly. Touching a finger to her clit, he let the movement of his thrusts provide the friction she needed on the throbbing bundle of nerves.

Her clit burned. Her pussy clenched. Her anus gripped.

Electric pulses centered between her legs and those devastating ripples began. Screaming mindlessly at the total loss of control, she involuntarily pushed back.

And went over.

Her entire body jolted as the sparks of pleasure spread and she screamed.

Wave after wave of the pleasure shook her. Spasms of indescribable ecstasy washed over her. She heard Jackson's growl and knew he'd also found his own pleasure.

His cock pulsed inside her and she could barely make out his words.

"So fucking incredible."

He slowly withdrew his finger and she groaned. She couldn't keep from tightening on his cock as it slipped from her dripping pussy. He covered her body with his, wrapping his arms around her as they lay spooned on his bed.

His lips moved over her neck and shoulder as he murmured softly to her, stroking her still trembling body.

"I love you, Sam."

The words spilled from him over and over as he held her. He knew the scene from earlier would replay in his mind over and over and he just wanted to forget it. He'd hoped that he would be able to make love to her tonight. He wanted to wipe all traces of the other man's touch from her mind.

She'd responded so beautifully and knew that she would go off like a firecracker when he and his brother took her together. With one filling her pussy and the other in that incredibly tight ass, all three of them would find pleasure like never before.

If only Shayne would let go.

He'd been extremely disappointed when Shayne hadn't joined them. Sure, it would be nice if each of them could spend time making love to her alone, but he'd thought that after what happened today, Shayne would have followed them into the house. Instead, he'd gone back to the stable.

He knew his brother loved Samantha and just hoped he intended to do something about it. If not, he would still keep her for himself. He wouldn't give her up. When he walked in to that nightmare today, it had shocked the hell out of him to realize just how much he loved her. He and Shayne had talked for years about sharing a woman but if Shayne couldn't give Samantha what she needed, he would have to find someone else.

Although she'd tried to hide it, Jackson had seen the hurt in her eyes that Shayne hadn't joined them. He would have to talk to Shayne and tell his brother to figure out his feelings for Samantha. He would have to either commit to her or walk away. Jackson couldn't stand to see her hurt again.

Hearing Samantha's even breathing, he smiled. She'd fallen asleep in his arms. After a brief trip to the bathroom, he eased back into bed, careful not to wake her. He reached down for the blanket to cover them both, settling her more firmly against him. When she cuddled against him, he smiled again and let himself drift off.

* * * *

She couldn't escape his grip. He held her too tightly and she knew he wanted to hurt her. She fought him, kicking and thrashing, trying to get free, but couldn't.

His grip tightened and she could feel his breath on her neck.

No! He would hurt her. He would push into her, invade her, taking something that she didn't want to give. She already knew the pain, knew how it would burn. She knew the helplessness she would feel.

No! No! No!

She fought against the arms holding her, couldn't understand the frantic words said against her ear as she fought.

She had to get away!

Samantha!

A deep voice boomed, startling her and cutting through the fog in her mind.

Her eyes popped open as she felt herself lifted effortlessly and then pressed tightly against a wall of heat, which wrapped around her.

"It's okay, baby. I've got you. Nobody's gonna hurt you ever again. Wake up, baby. Wake up for me."

Samantha jerked in surprise to find herself in Shayne's arms as he stood next to Jackson's bed. Remembering her nightmare, she buried her face in his throat, still trembling in reaction. Her arms tightened around his neck. Her legs wrapped around his waist, absorbing his heat. When his cock jumped against her bottom, she realized he was naked.

One huge hand under her bottom held her tightly against his chest while the other stroked her back. "You're okay, baby. I've got you. Nobody's here but Jackson and me."

She nodded, sneaking a peek at Jackson. He knelt on the bed, his face tight with concern. She tightened her grip on Shayne as she reached out a hand to Jackson. "I'm sorry. I didn't mean to scare you."

Jackson gripped her hand. "Are you okay, honey? I couldn't wake you up."

She nodded again. "I'm fine. I'm okay." She took a shuddering breath. "I was dreaming about today."

"Come on, Jackson." Shayne's deep voice rumbled softly. "My bed's bigger."

Shayne carried Samantha out of Jackson's bedroom and into his. Samantha looked over Shayne's shoulder to see Jackson following them, smiling in satisfaction.

Before they could get to the bed, Samantha leaned back to look up at Shayne. "Stop."

Shayne halted abruptly in the middle of the room. "What is it? Do you have to go to the bathroom?"

Samantha shook her head. "No, but I can't sleep with you."

Shayne frowned at her. "Why not? Are you scared I'll hurt you?"

She shook her head sadly. "The only way that you could hurt me is by doing this when you don't care about me. I appreciate you holding me and waking me up from my dream, but I know that you don't want me the way Jackson does. I know you're scared to care about me and I can't get involved with someone who doesn't want any more than just sex."

Her voice wobbled and she had to clear her throat before she could continue, avoiding his gaze by staring at his naked chest. "I love you, Shayne. But it would kill me to have only parts of you."

"You think I don't love you?"

Samantha looked up at Shayne's incredulous tone.

A heartbeat later, he'd pulled her back against him, burying his face in her throat. "I love you so much I can't stand it. I love you so much that after I punched that man today, I wanted to do it again and again. He touched you. He hurt you. Now he's giving you nightmares and I want to beat the hell out of him all over again."

His arms tightened around her, almost crushing her to him and still she pulled him tighter. "You love me?"

He leaned back to look at her, his face tight. "Of course, I love you. How could anyone not love you? But I'm too rough for someone like you. It would kill me if I hurt you. I don't know what to do for you."

She said the words she couldn't say before. "Love me."

Samantha caressed his cheek, sliding a glance at Jackson, who smiled as he waited in the bed for them. "The only way you could hurt me is by not loving me. I love you just the way you are. Your strength saved me today and you held me after my nightmare. You hold me, and you pour me milk. You are gentle with me. The only thing I want you to do for me is love me."

Shayne smiled. The emotion in his eyes nearly undid her. "I already do."

When his mouth covered hers, Samantha knew she'd found paradise. She had no doubt now that both men loved her as much as she loved them. She couldn't wait to start their future together.

"Are you two coming to bed or are you going to stay there all night?"

Shayne lifted his head at Jackson's amused tone. "We're coming to bed."

When Shayne moved toward the bed, Samantha bit her lip worriedly. "What if I have another nightmare. Maybe I should go sleep on the sofa."

Shayne lay on the bed, settling her on top of his big body. "No. You sleep right here." He reached over and turned off the light.

Lying on top of Shayne, her legs on either side of his waist, and his cock touching her bottom, Samantha knew sleep would be impossible. She could already feel her pussy weep and raised herself just enough to rub her nipples against his chest.

Shayne lay with his eyes closed as she began to move against him.

When she felt Jackson's hand on her thigh, she looked over to find him watching her in the nearly dark room. Using only the tips of his fingers, he grazed over her thigh and down to the back of her knee before moving back up again, leaving a trail of tingling heat wherever he touched.

"My stomach is getting wet."

Samantha looked up at Shayne and smiled.

His lips curved. "Somebody's dripping all over me."

His hands tightened on her waist as he lifted her, slowly lowering her inch by inch onto his cock.

Samantha groaned at the wonderful fullness and clenched on the steely thickness. Facing Jackson, she saw his pleased smile as he reached out to caress her breast. She shifted, groaning at the wonderful fullness of Shayne's hard cock inside her.

The sound of a drawer being opened and closed made her turn her head to see Shayne squirting lube onto his finger. She gasped. "What are you going to do?"

Shayne recapped the lube and slid his hand to her bottom, pulling her down onto his chest and working the lube into her tight opening. Groaning, she tried to sit up but he held her down as he slid a thick finger into her, his big hand covering most of her buttocks as he held her in place.

Shayne's thick shaft jumped inside her. She felt Jackson move in behind her, making soft erotic promises in her ear as his arms came around to cup her breasts.

When Shayne's slick finger slid out of her bottom, Jackson's cock quickly replaced it. He pressed the head of it against her tight opening and she cried out at the pinch as he breached it.

"That's it, sweetheart. Let me in your tight ass."

Shayne held her hips firmly as Jackson pressed his cock little by little into her bottom, stretching her anus and making it burn deliciously.

"Oh! I'm so full."

"You're about to get fuller," Jackson groaned harshly as he steadily worked his length into her.

She felt as though she would burst, so full her mind went blank as her lovers established a rhythm, their strokes stretching her deliciously.

She shifted slightly off of Shayne's chest, her head thrown back as she gave herself up to the pleasure. The sounds of their lovemaking sent her even higher. The deep growls and erotic praise from her lovers made her feel even more desired.

Her hands fisted on Shayne's chest. His thick muscles beneath them felt hard as they shifted as he moved her body over his. Looking down, she met his eyes, which glittered in the small sliver of light coming through the window.

"I love you, baby." His deep growl sounded so highly erotic, she shivered. "You'll never get away from us now."

Samantha moaned when the pad of his thumb touched her clit. Her answer became lost in a moan as waves of pleasure washed over her. Her pussy and anus clenched hard and fast on the thick cocks thrusting relentlessly inside her.

Her cries of release and her lovers' harsh groans filled the room as they all found their pleasure. The hands on her firmed, holding her steady as they held their pulsing cocks deep inside her.

Jackson's arms came around her and he buried his face in her hair. "Oh, Sam. I love you so damned much."

"I love you, too." Overcome with emotion, her voice wobbled. "I love you both so much."

"Come here, baby."

Jackson released her so Shayne could lower her to his chest. Wrapping his big arms around her, he stroked her back. His arms tightened, holding her close when she groaned as Jackson withdrew from her. With a lingering kiss on her shoulder, Jackson got off the bed and headed for the bathroom.

Shayne ran a hand through her hair. "I never thought I'd have a woman like you."

Samantha lifted her head to smile up at him. "I never thought I'd have a man like you." She paused, watching him through her lashes. "You wouldn't really pull my jeans down and spank me, would you?"

Shayne lifted his head to look down at her. His eyes blazed and she felt his cock jump inside her. "Every time you disobey me," he warned darkly.

Samantha smothered a groan as her pussy clenched on him in response. "I might have to be bad," she grinned at him daringly, running a nail over his nipple.

Shayne chuckled, a sound she hoped she would hear with increasing regularity. He ran a hand threateningly over her bottom. "Be careful, little girl. I never did punish you for leaving the ranch when you were told not to."

Samantha giggled. "I'm not scared of you."

Shayne grinned, taking Samantha's breath away. "No, you're not, are you? But that doesn't mean I won't spank you if you deserve it. Go to sleep, baby." He gave her bottom a light slap as he dropped his head on the pillow.

"Spank?" Jackson chuckled as he came back to bed. "What the hell did I miss?"

Shayne never opened his eyes. "I owe Samantha a spanking."

"Now?" Jackson asked hopefully.

"Tomorrow. She's going to need to rest up for it. Once her ass is red, I'm going to fuck it nice and slow."

Samantha gasped. "Really? You're not afraid you'll hurt me?"

"Really. And the only thing that's going to hurt is your ass if you disobey me again. Now go to sleep. I'm going to need all of my energy to deal with you."

Samantha and Jackson smiled at each other, still holding hands as they fell asleep.

This time when they slept, nobody stirred until late the next morning.

When Samantha did her best to be *really* bad.

THE END

www.SirenPublishing.com/LeahBrooke

ABOUT THE AUTHOR

Leah Brooke has always loved to read and is addicted to happily ever afters. A bit of a daydreamer, for years she's written stories for her own amusement.

At her mother's encouragement, she decided to send one in.

Her first manuscript was born.

Since then, she spends most of her time working on the happily ever afters that keep racing through her mind.

Siren Publishing, Inc.
www.SirenPublishing.com

LaVergne, TN USA
12 February 2010
172967LV00006B/40/P